The police were using clubs now to disperse us. There was a lot of shouting behind me and a scream. Suddenly gunfire rang out from the jeep. They were shooting randomly over my head across the river. I heard two bursts of rapid machine-gun fire of about twenty seconds each.

I started running across the bridge. "Fatmira, get down! Get down!" I screamed.

But it was too late. She had already fallen. I threw myself on her and shook her to try to rouse her, but she wouldn't wake up. Big hands pried me off her body. From her hand I quickly took the folded piece of paper and slipped it into my pocket. I didn't want the Serb police to find the poem on her.

As the police pulled me away, I could see blood and a black bullet hole burned through her denim jacket in the middle of her back. Someone had turned her over. Her face was white. Blood trickled from the corner of her mouth.

I was screaming her name and wouldn't stop. The police brushed me aside and loaded her into their jeep. I grabbed on to the door handle and tried to climb in, too. "Let me go with you!" I screamed. "Don't take her away. I can make her better."

The police pushed me away and quickly drove through the crowd.

ALICE MEAD

ADEM'S CROSS

LAUREL-LEAF
BOOKS

Published by
Bantam Doubleday Dell Books for Young Readers
a division of
Bantam Doubleday Dell Publishing Group, Inc.
1540 Broadway
New York, New York 10036

*The author wishes to gratefully acknowledge Dr. Steven L.
Burg, Professor of Politics, Brandeis University, for his critical
reading of the manuscript.*

*Most of the places mentioned in this book are real. However,
both Adem's village and the lake to which he escapes at the
end are fictional.*

Visit us on the Web! www.bdd.com

Educators and librarians, visit the BDD Teacher's Resource
Center at www.bdd.com/teachers

ISBN: 0-440-22735-6

RL: 5.0

Reprinted by arrangement with Farrar Straus Giroux

Printed in the United States of America

May 1998

10 9 8 7 6 5 4 3

OPM

To the children of the former Yugoslavia,
in the hope that one day they will have
the chance to study and play again,
and to Erleta, Driton, and Nermina,
who have helped me on my way

PRONUNCIATION GUIDE

Burek   *Boor-EK*
Dobro vece   *DOH-broh VEY-cheh*
Flie   *Flee-AH*
Gëzuar   *Geh-ZU-ar*
Milos   *MEE-losh*
Milosevic   *Mee-LOSH-a-vich*
Mirë   *MEE-ruh*
Pristina   *Prish-TEE-na*
Sar Mountains   *Shar Mountains*
Vojvodina   *Voy-vo-DEE-na*

AUTHOR'S NOTE

Yugoslavia was a country in Eastern Europe until 1991. Since the end of World War II, it had been ruled by a strong leader named Tito. It was made up of six republics—Serbia; Macedonia; Bosnia and Herzegovina; Croatia; Slovenia; Montenegro—and two less independent provinces, Kosovo and Vojvodina. Serbia was the largest republic, while Kosovo, where this story is set, was the poorest province in Yugoslavia.

Tito died in 1980. At that time the ethnic Albanians of Kosovo were growing more and more unhappy with the quality of their lives. These people made up about 85 percent of the population in Kosovo; the rest were Serbs. In 1981, Albanian university students and many others began to demonstrate for Kosovo's independence.

The Yugoslav government in Belgrade had a very large army and police force. It responded to the Albanian students' demonstrations with beatings, imprisonment, and a crackdown on civil liberties. Many military police were moved to the region to keep order.

But the Albanians continued to seek rights and independence. Every time there was a demonstration, more soldiers and special police arrived in Kosovo. Every time they arrived, they brought weapons and stayed. Other republics of Yugoslavia watched the violence in Kosovo nervously to see what would happen, but no one offered to help.

Slobodan Milosevic, the leader of Serbia, wanted to seize power during this confusing time. First he turned to the impoverished Albanian people in Kosovo. Serbs, he said, had the right to ancient landholdings there from hundreds of years ago. He reminded them that Kosovo had been part of the Serbian heartland until the Ottoman Turks defeated the Serbs in the 1389 Battle of Kosovo. Refusing to convert to the religion of Islam (as the Albanians and Bosnians did), the Serbs (Orthodox Christians) had been expelled from the area, where ethnic Albanians multiplied. Now the Serbs would reclaim their territory.

In 1989, Milosevic held a rally and declared his intention to consolidate Serbian power in Belgrade under his control. At that point, the other republics of Yugoslavia prepared to secede. That led, in 1991, to the outbreak of terrible wars with various Serbian factions in the provinces of Bosnia and Croatia.

Milosevic's method was to take over Yugoslavia's radio, newspapers, and TV. Then the media broadcast scary stories about Muslims in both Bosnia and Kosovo. According to the broadcasts, Muslim Albanians in Kosovo were "murderers and beasts, terrorists who kill Serbs in their beds." Milosevic said he would have to send more tanks and soldiers to Kosovo to keep the "unity" of Yugoslavia and to protect Serbs from those monsters. He created an atmosphere of fear between Albanians and Serbs, who, despite different languages, religions, and customs, had lived together peacefully for years. Milosevic also encouraged outbursts of local violence, which he then magnified in reports on TV.

In March 1989, Serbian tanks and helicopters surrounded

the Kosovo government buildings. Milosevic suspended the province's constitution. In its place, he installed the "special military measures" needed for total control of the unarmed Albanians.

The region now contains 60,000 special police and soldiers. According to the 1995 United States State Department Country Report, "Milosevic wields strong control over the Serbian police, a heavily armed force of perhaps 100,000, which is guilty of extensive, brutal, and systematic human rights abuses."

The Albanians formed a democratic alliance, held elections, and used nonviolence to protest these policies, but so far attempts at negotiations between Milosevic and Albanian leaders have failed.

Meanwhile, in Kosovo, there is no news from the outside world. Thousands of families subsist on bread and eggs. Factories and banks are closed. Many Albanian men and boys have left the region to escape abuse and to try to find jobs in other countries, while Serbian refugees from warring parts of Bosnia and Croatia have been moved in.

Neither Albanians nor Serbs in Kosovo want war, but no one sees a way out. This story starts in September 1993— more than four and a half years after the military crackdown by the Yugoslav army. The protagonist is one of the one million ethnic Albanian children in Kosovo. His story is typical of the violence and turmoil suffered by children all across the former Yugoslavia.

ADEM'S CROSS

ONE

A year ago, in August 1992, my aunt died suddenly of a cough. It might have been cancer, my mother said. But my aunt was afraid to go to the hospital because of the Serb doctors, so we never found out the cause. My Uncle Sal was left with four children. To make things easier at their home, my older cousin, Besim, came to live with us. He was sixteen then. I was thirteen. He brought their cow, too. It was smaller than ours, and mostly white, with tan spots. Before I realized it, I was taking care of both cows, ours and theirs, while Besim lay on the sofa pillows inside the house, watching MTV on the Belgrade station.

Besim didn't care much about daytime activities. He was waiting for the sun to set. Every evening, when the air grew cooler, we always, all of us, went out walking through towns and villages all over Kosovo, meeting friends, talking. We continued to do this even after the Serbs came. We wouldn't stop it, not even for them.

Before he went out at night, Besim took a shower, put on after-shave, and then put on his tight black jeans. He spent half an hour in front of the mirror, checking himself from every angle. While Besim was in our small bathroom behind the kitchen after dinner, my mother scrubbed the table and hung the tablecloth out on the line. My father sat at the kitchen table and hooted with laughter. "You look like Elvis Presley," he joked.

I watched jealously from the doorway. If I had dressed up like Besim, my father would have been angry and told me to stop showing off. It was obvious that he liked Besim more than me.

When Besim thought he looked perfect, he stood in front of my father, his hands on his hips. "Well?" he demanded.

"You'll have a line of girls following you, stretching from here to the mountains," my father said.

Besim laughed and went out. I started to go with him.

"No, not you. A boy his age needs some privacy. You can keep your grandfather company," my father said to me. "Sit."

I sat on the front step. Behind me the red sun was setting over Albania and the mountains. In front of me were the fields, and to the south the Sar Mountains looked soft and pink in the sunset. The Sar Mountains separated us from Macedonia. Black crows rose up out of the apple trees lining the road. Then, like a flapped dark cloth, they resettled again in the shadowy branches. Their cawing died away. I picked up a rock and tossed it angrily down the path.

"Hey!"

My sister Fatmira had come up behind me. I'd been so busy sulking I hadn't even heard her.

"What's wrong, Adem?" She crouched down next to me.

"Nothing. Papa likes Besim better than me, that's all."

"That's crazy. No he doesn't." She laughed.

"Then why does he make me take care of Besim's cow? Why does he let Besim go out alone dressed up like that?"

"He wants to be nice to Besim because Aunt Linda died. That's all," Fatmira said, giving my shoulder a little shake.

I turned and looked into her dark brown eyes. Her eyes had an extra sparkle in them tonight, and I wasn't sure why. "Is something up?" I asked suspiciously.

Fatmira was sixteen. During the past few weeks, she'd gone into Prizren from our small village several times, but I didn't know the reason. It was the first time she'd kept a secret from me. Maybe she had a boyfriend.

She stood up. "Of course not," she said lightly. "I'll see you in the park in a little while."

I rested my chin on my knees. Maybe that *was* the reason my father babied Besim, but I still felt jealous. I wished I were seventeen, too, and ready to start life on my own.

Finally my grandfather was ready. He walked down

the dirt lane slowly, with both hands folded behind his back. Step by step, methodically, we approached the stony street that led to the center of the village. Each person we passed he stopped to greet, and I had to say hello, too, politely, or I'd hear about it later.

I was so bored. And since tomorrow was the first day of school, I was also nervous. No one knew exactly what would happen to us on the first day, but it never passed without violence. I tried not to think about it.

We reached the little park at the center of the village. Two girls, arm in arm, wearing lipstick and carefully permed hair, stood with their eyes cast demurely down, murmuring together in low voices. Even though they weren't exactly looking at him, I knew—everyone knew—that they were intensely aware of Besim. He stood near them, one foot raised on the park bench, playing an imaginary guitar, strumming and flinging his head back. He had all the moves down perfectly.

My grandfather frowned to see girls unescorted like that. My grandmother hadn't even come out. She spent most of her time at home because that was the wish of my grandfather. That way there was always someone in the house.

"Ah! Good evening!" my grandfather called out to an old friend.

They had been soldiers together in World War II. Albanian Partisans, claiming to be some of the fiercest fighters found anywhere. They had chased the Croats and the Nazis from Albania. Tonight Grandpa's friend wore his old blue military jacket. They were talking about

Grandpa's brother, who had been a brave soldier. He lived in Albania, in a city called Elbasan. We had cousins there, but it had been years since we'd been allowed to see them.

"A lovely evening," my grandfather's friend said to us, taking Grandpa's hand in both of his. "How are you?"

"Good, good," murmured Grandpa.

I waited, not as patiently as I should have. I looked up at the mountains. Once we met our Elbasan cousins in Macedonia, when I was about eight or nine. But now the border with Albania was closed, and we couldn't see our families anymore. Now even to say the word "Albania" was very dangerous.

"And how is your family?"

"Oh, fine, fine."

What lies, I thought. Every night the same routine. How are you? Oh, fine. How could we be fine? Any of us. School would start tomorrow, and something would happen. Why did we have to pretend it wouldn't?

Mosquitoes bit my bare arms. I slapped them hard. My grandfather frowned at me and moved off slowly with his friend. I trailed behind, full of frustration. We could say nothing. We were trapped, surrounded by Serb tanks and machine guns. We could only wait for things to get better and try to live life as normally as possible.

Suddenly two blue military jeeps, loaded with Serb soldiers and machine guns, rattled down the hill and parked at the edge of the square. The soldiers passed around a pack of cigarettes to one another, then leaned back in their seats and blew smoke into the darkening purple sky of the early September evening. They watched us with lazy eyes and flicked ashes into the street.

I stared at them, even though I knew I shouldn't. We were locked in a war of nerves, no matter how quiet the village seemed. What would tomorrow bring? I felt dread tingling in my arms, down into my fingers. I closed my eyes for a moment and pushed the feeling away by force. Don't let them scare you, I told myself.

I stayed behind my grandfather, waiting for Fatmira to come. Some girls from my class were standing nearby, glancing at me and then at Besim and giggling. I rolled my eyes and they burst out laughing.

Another of my grandfather's friends approached. He held out his hand to me.

"How are you, Adem?"

"Oh, good, good," I muttered, as I was expected to.

I saw my mother and my two sisters walking with Uncle Sal down the hill to join us in the park. My mother and uncle moved off to talk with my grandfather and his friends. My sisters began to walk with me. Fatmira took one glance at me and laughed immediately. She could see how I felt.

"Are you ready for school tomorrow? Are you ready for the Stork?"

She tucked her hands under her armpits and flapped her elbows, making fun of our tall, skinny English teacher, Mr. Gashi. She wanted to make me laugh because she knew that deep down I was scared.

In spite of my fear, I had to laugh. My little sister, Pranvera, leaned her head against Fatmira's shoulder. "What?" she asked. "What's funny?"

Fatmira hugged her. "We are laughing about our teacher, Mr. Gashi."

I glanced over at the soldiers to see if they'd heard us. If we laughed too much, they might start to come toward us.

"Aren't you scared, Fatmira? The first day of school, who knows what will happen," I said.

Fatmira frowned at me and shook her head, indicating that we shouldn't frighten Pranvera, who was only ten. The soldiers usually teargassed the older Albanian children. Most of the time they left the little ones alone.

"This September will be different, Adem."

"What do you mean? You mean the soldiers won't come to our school?"

She shook her head. "You'll see. You have to be patient."

TWO

Several times I'd been teargassed—we all had—at our parallel village school, where we went to be taught the Albanian language and customs. We Albanian kids were kept on one floor. The Serb kids used the other. We didn't talk to or even look at one another. We used to be playmates, but those days were long over. Although it had been less than five years, so much had changed since the tanks first came.

Every September, on the first day of school, we could count on tear gas. Midmorning, the Serb special police always came and stood in the road. They shot tear-gas pellets into the school yard and into the open windows of the building. The windows weren't really open. It was just that there was no glass in them. The Serbs had broken all the windows on the first floor of the school so that we would be cold. Flies were free to come and go. We had no chairs to sit on and no heat or electricity either. It had been years since we'd had books to read.

The kids in the back of the classroom saw the jeeps first. Their bouncing tires raised a cloud of dust in the village street.

"The police, Mr. Gashi," Avni said. "They're coming!"

The other kids in the back of the room, including me, snickered nervously. It was ironic for Avni to tell us the police were coming because his father was an informer for the Serbs. In a village as small as ours, everyone knew who the informers were.

Mr. Gashi stepped carefully through the crowd of kids sitting wedged in tightly on the floor.

"All right," he said after gazing out the shattered window.

Jagged shards of glass still stood in the broken frames, while outside pieces of glass lay in tiny fragments on the playground. No one had ever bothered to pick them up or sweep them away.

It seemed that Mr. Gashi had forgotten there were thirty of us in the room behind him. Then he said, "Take your jackets—"

But it was too late. The police began shooting. Pop. Pop pop. Pop!

One canister landed in our room. We covered our eyes and faces as best we could, stupidly vowing not to move.

"Run!" Mr. Gashi shouted. "Run down to the stream. Someone will come for you later."

The cloud of gas filled the room, burning our eyes and

throats. We ran every time. We had to. I don't know why we bothered to promise ourselves that this year we would stay. Of course we ran. We ran across my family's cornfield toward the stream. Then we sat by the edge of the stream, coughing, telling jokes, and making fun of the soldiers.

"Space aliens," I called them. "Frog faces in gas masks."

"You Serbs are not human. You couldn't be, or else how could you do this to schoolchildren?" Besim yelled.

We sang songs about driving them out of Kosovo so life could go back to the way it was before.

Besim liked to show off in front of the others. He acted like a know-it-all. "Well, don't worry," he said. "September's always the worst month. After this, things will get better."

I glanced at Fatmira and sighed with disgust. Besim often repeated whatever he heard the grownups say. My father praised him for that.

"Life will go back to the way it was before. We just have to be patient," he said.

I coughed loudly to drown him out and pretended to retch into my cupped hands. Fatmira nudged me to stop. I looked at her. She gave me a little frown. Why wasn't she jealous of Besim, as I was? How did she stay so calm? No matter what happened, she seemed to have no fear.

"The way it was before"—every day we talked about this. "Before" meant before the Serb army had occupied us, when we had our own government. Not even five years ago, we could do what we wanted, just as we had under Tito. He was a good guy, everyone said. At least he had kept peace in Yugoslavia and given us Albanians some rights so that we could think and decide a few things for ourselves.

"Besim, you're such a liar," I said. "How do you know that will happen?"

I wanted the other kids to stop watching him. Before he moved in with us, I had been the oldest boy in our house. Being the oldest boy was an important role in Albanian families. Someday, you would become the head of the family, and that gave you certain privileges while you were growing up. Besim leaned over and gave me a shove. I shook him off.

"Don't fight. Let's sing rock songs," Fatmira suggested. Some of the girls were crying, and the younger boys looked as if they were about to.

While we were singing loudly by the muddy little stream where the cows often waded, the police were inside the school beating our teachers and our headmaster. Sometimes they took the headmaster to the police station, where they beat him for days. Many headmasters had died that way. So we sang "Great Balls of Fire" by Jerry Lee Lewis and then Chubby Checker songs. Then Beatles. Anything to pass the time without thinking too much. The silly songs were best because then we could act really wild and crazy.

As I sang, I began coughing again and holding my eyes. They stung terribly this time. I wondered if the police had added some new chemical to the tear gas to make it feel worse.

While the Serb kids heard the thuds and screams from down below, they had to stay in their classrooms and pretend nothing was going on. In that way, everything that happened to us happened to them, too.

How stupid this all was!

The sun beat down on us. It felt like a hot hand pressing on the top of my head, and for a moment I thought I might go crazy in the glare of it. I wished for soft gray clouds like cushions that I could sink into.

I squinted my eyes to look across the field. Our cornfield was dry. We had had almost no rain all summer long. It had been the third dry summer in a row. The cornstalks were an ugly, dull yellow from the drought, more like stalks of stiffened, yellowed newspaper than like plants.

At the edge of the field near our house, a row of sunflowers I had planted last spring stood tall and tilted at odd angles, weighed down with heavy, blackened flowers. My grandmother wanted me to cut them down. She said it was a bad omen to leave black sunflowers standing. It gave her bad dreams. Maybe I would cut them down now. Why not? I stood up. I wanted to do something rash and impulsive. I could easily tear the sunflower stalks up by the roots.

"Get down," said Fatmira. "You're acting crazy, Adem."

I grinned at her. "Look who's talking. Didn't you say this September would be different? I don't see anything different."

She smiled back. "I'll tell you later."

"Good," I said and flopped back in the dry grass. "Tell the police I'm sleeping."

Fatmira jumped up and led some of the younger girls over to where she was sitting. Slowly and gently, she began to braid one girl's hair.

From near some alder bushes, our two cows watched us. All the students were sitting on the edge of the stream bank, legs dangling, ready to drop down low if the police came toward us. But they wouldn't. They never came after us—too much running. By now they would be getting tired from giving beatings. It was hard work to beat someone for ten minutes.

As time passed, the boys started to talk. "One day, the Americans will come. Their President will send tanks to help us. Then you'll see the Serbs run. They aren't like us, brave and organized. They don't have solidarity, the way we do. We fight with our minds and hearts. They are a pack of animals. Look what they did to Bosnia."

Bosnia.

This always stopped the talking. We saw the terrible war in Bosnia on Serb TV. They showed it to us often as an example of our future, of what would happen to us Albanians if we didn't give them our province of Kosovo.

"Don't worry. The Turks are sending weapons into Bosnia. Maybe they will send them here," Besim said. In a year, he would be drafted by the Serbs to fight for them.

"Shut up," I said.

Over and over, everyone said the same thing. I was so tired of hearing about the Turks and their weapons. It was pure rumor, an excuse for the Serbs to search our houses whenever they wanted to, usually in the middle of the night. Besides, Besim shouldn't talk about it in front of Avni, who would tell his father.

Avni's father had become an informer because they'd been so poor. They'd had no food. Now they weren't poor. For the first day of school, Avni wore tight new blue jeans that cost one hundred and fifty German marks and came from Switzerland, smuggled in over the mountains in Montenegro.

I felt a sharp pang of pity for Avni in his stiff new jeans. What good were they? I let a wave of anger flow through me, making me reckless.

"Come on. Why are we afraid of them? Let's go back to school. I want to live normally," I said. I jumped up.

Fatmira grabbed my arm. "No, the jeeps are still there. If they see us coming, they may be tempted to beat the teachers some more so that we can watch. You never think of others, Adem."

It was true, what she said. I was impatient, jealous, and angry. Restless, too. I couldn't help it.

My sister had power over me that no one else had. She was like my mother. She had raised me while my mother nursed my younger brother, Angel, who was handicapped. Now he lived at a school for retarded children on the road to Pristina, the capital of Kosovo.

Besides him and my younger sister, Pranvera, there was the baby, Halil, who was two. Five children was not such a big family in Kosovo. Some people had twelve, enough for a soccer team and a referee. Some had more.

So we sat by the stream. It was filled with silty, brown

mud and was very shallow. Our fields were slowly washing away because we'd had to cut so much firewood during the past few years. We had a power plant in Kosovo, but the Serbs used it to sell electricity to other parts of the country. Sometimes—usually in the mornings—we did have electricity. But at night, we never knew what to expect. People came from as far as Prizren to cut wood here to take back to town.

We sang more songs and told jokes, waiting and waiting, trying to make one another laugh. Every time someone got serious, we joked and got him or her laughing again. After the Beatles, we sang rap songs from MTV. Then Besim grabbed a branch and played guitar with it, showing off and flinging his long hair around like a heavy-metal guitarist.

Finally the math teacher came across the field to get us, walking carefully in her high heels and skirt.

"What happened?" I jumped to my feet. "Did they take anyone to jail?"

Mrs. Mehmeti rubbed my hair. "You are incorrigible," she said.

"Well, did they?" I had to know.

"Yes."

"The headmaster?"

"Yes."

"What about you? Did they beat you?"

"Does it look like they did? No. Just Mr. Hajrizi—as an example to us."

At school, we sat in the dirt of the school yard. We didn't bother to go inside. Mr. Gashi gave us a lecture.

He stood before us, looking very tired. His eyes were half-closed and his voice sleepy.

"Our yearly pep talk," I whispered to Besim.

Besim glared at me.

"We must continue to be brave," Mr. Gashi said. "I want all of you to come to school all year. Every day. It's important that we show them that we won't give up. We have a right to teach and learn in our own language. They can't take that away from us, no matter how often they beat us or use tear gas. You know September is a bad month. Every year, with the start of school, we go through this. But things will calm down. Our lives will get better soon. We must hope for that and go on with our unity and resistance. The politicians assure us that their diplomatic methods are working."

"When are the American tanks coming?" I yelled from the back.

There was dead silence. Everyone turned around to stare at me in shock. It was unthinkable to yell this out with Serb children and police nearby. But why not? Our parents and teachers told us tanks were coming. I was tired of waiting, that was all. Mr. Gashi said nothing.

I shrugged. "I just wondered," I said. A few kids laughed.

Upstairs on the second floor, I saw a Serb boy named Milos looking out the window at me. We stared at each other. He was waiting for me to look away first, but I wouldn't. I wondered what he'd heard upstairs while the police were beating our headmaster. Milos and I used to be best friends.

"Now you are dismissed. I will see you tomorrow," Mr. Gashi said. We all scrambled to our feet and brushed the dust off our clothes.

Up at the window, I saw Milos give me the finger. When we played soccer together, we'd been unstoppable. Now he was on a team, but I wasn't allowed to play anymore. No Albanian children were. I gave Milos a big, sarcastic smile and he turned away.

School got out at eleven, to leave time for the second shift of Albanian kids to come in. I let everyone push out of the school yard gate ahead of me, and I walked home alone. So school was over for today. And what had I learned?

As I left the school yard, I yelled out, "What's for homework?" But I didn't expect an answer. I was fourteen, that was all, and grownups annoyed me.

THREE

As soon as I got home, I had to clean the cow shed. I raked out the dirty hay and tossed forkfuls of fresh, dry hay inside. The shed was crowded now, with two cows in it, and a dusty scattering of hay fell on the cows' backs. I sneezed and pitched in some more. The cows were glad to be out of the hot noontime sun. I got them each a big bucket of water from the well.

While they drank, I swept the hay off their backs and then patted them. I scratched my big, brown cow under the ears and laid my cheek on her neck and hugged her. I missed Milos and our old soccer games. I always used to be goalie because I wasn't afraid to dive headlong into the dirt to block a kick. Milos had played forward, and he'd been just as wild. Someday, if I ever managed to escape to Italy, I would buy a thousand soccer balls.

"Adem!"

"What?"

I jumped back. I didn't want anyone to see me hugging a cow. But it was only Fatmira. I didn't mind what she saw. Now that Milos and I rarely saw each other, my older sister had become my best friend. I felt I had to hide my feelings from everyone else, but not from her.

"Listen! I need to go into Prizren tomorrow."

I glanced at her. Her voice was tense and excited.

"Why?" I asked uneasily.

"You don't want to go?"

"No, no. I'll go. Of course I'll go." I would do anything to break up the monotony of our lives.

"Right after school."

"Really?" I asked. "Why not wait until a little later, when it's cooler?"

Fatmira was staring out the doorway of the shed, across the big cornfield to where my father was cutting hay with some neighbors and my Uncle Sal.

"Okay," she said. "At three o'clock."

I narrowed my eyes. She was never tense and nervous like this.

"What's going on?" I asked again. "Are you meeting a boy?"

She looked at me as if measuring me in some way. I gave her a big grin to prove my loyalty. She laughed.

"Okay," she said. "Today there was a big demonstration in Macedonia by Albanian university students. They had been planning it all summer to support us on the first day of school."

I frowned. "How do you know this?"

"Because this summer I joined a group of activists in Prizren. But that doesn't matter. What matters is to keep the chain going. We have to face the fact that the adults here are too tired at this point. We, the younger people, have to seize this opportunity and show the Serbs that Albanian unity extends across borders."

Fatmira's eyes glittered with excitement. I was just about to ask her what my parents thought of all this when I heard Besim come into the courtyard.

"Ssh!" she whispered. Then she turned around and stepped out of the shed. "Besim, Adem and I are going to Prizren at three tomorrow if you want to come."

"Yeah, okay."

I put down the pitchfork and picked up a small straw broom and swept the cement steps in the courtyard free of dust and bits of hay. Fatmira was unpegging the laundry from the clothesline. Besim was doing nothing. I felt very uneasy after my talk with Fatmira. Who was she going to meet when we got to Prizren? What kind of friends did she have there? How long had she been keeping this secret from me?

Close to the borders of both Albania and Macedonia, Prizren was always very tense and full of special police and soldiers. The Serbs said they had to keep these heavily armed police there because the city was full of Albanian radicals, people who wanted an open war with the Serbs to get back control of Kosovo. We had talked about it many times—Fatmira wasn't for war at all. She was for free expression, and for peaceful resistance. She hated weapons, I reminded myself. So I had nothing to worry about.

I went inside, and my mother and Pranvera fixed Besim and me a lunch of flaky-crusted *burek* filled with feta cheese. For once there was plenty of food, and I ate too much and then drank a large Coke. My stomach felt like a tightly stretched balloon, so I had to lie down for a while.

But while I rested on one of the living room sofas, I fretted about my conversation with Fatmira. Well, she was older than I; I decided she knew what she was doing. I pushed the uneasy thoughts from my mind. I repeated to myself what all Albanians told themselves, "Someday soon, things will get better."

Our family had a car, but there was no money for gasoline, and, anyway, we had a flat tire. So no one had been able to drive the car for months, and it sat out under the apple trees at the edge of the field.

When they went to Prizren, my parents and grandparents used the horse-drawn farm cart. The children walked. It took us over two hours. But that didn't really matter. After we finished our chores, what else did we have to do? Once we used to play soccer every afternoon under the apple trees behind the house. We'd stayed near the well when we played so we could get cool water when we got hot. Now we weren't allowed to play any organized sports.

People said the soldiers played soccer outside the army barracks. People said the Serb soldiers were even poorer than we were and didn't have enough to eat. Who knew if this was true?

The next afternoon, we set out about three o'clock, Fatmira, Besim, Pranvera, and I, walking down the long, sloping hill covered with row after row of grapevines. Far off, in the valley below, the orange-tiled rooftops and tall minarets of the mosques of Prizren crowded around the riverbed.

Halfway into town, we passed a flat stretch of gravel by the side of the road. Here some Gypsies camped every summer until winter came. No one bothered them much. No one knew exactly where they went in winter. Probably to Macedonia or Bulgaria. They helped with the grape harvest. They brought mounds of trash up from Prizren and burned garbage instead of firewood. They got some food from it, too.

People said the Gypsies liked the valleys of Prizren because there were so many wild animals still roaming the mountainsides here. They trapped foxes and bears and even wolves, people said, and sold them in Europe.

Maybe. I knew one of them, a man named Fikel. He said he came from Romania. That was where Transylvania was. He said "Dracula's castle" was nothing special, that there was a far better one built by Dracula, who was really Vlad the Impaler. I wished I could go see it. I liked Fikel. He'd traveled everywhere. The war in Bosnia hadn't stopped him one bit.

"Come on," said Fatmira impatiently.

We all hurried. She walked ahead of us, then took a folded piece of paper out of her pocket and read it silently. I had to find out what was going on.

"What's that?" I asked.

"Promise you won't tell Besim?" she asked.

"No! I hate that," I said. "I won't promise."

She looked at me sideways and smiled. We shared the same spirit in a way that our cousin Besim did not.

"All right," she said. "It's a poem. I'm reading it today. That's the secret."

A thrill of fear went through me. Poems were dangerous. Rebellious. And in Prizren!

"About what?" I persisted. "School?"

"No. It's about the river that runs through Prizren. The Serbs are planning to blow it up, to change its course. My poem is about the ancient Ottoman bridges. I love those bridges, Adem."

The bridges were very beautiful, five of them made of stone arches, built hundreds of years ago.

"When are they going to blow it up?" I asked. I couldn't understand this. It sounded so ridiculous.

"Sunday is what I heard," she said. "Today, at six o'clock, four high-school students from Prizren and I are going to read poems from the center of each bridge."

"You could get in trouble, Fatmira," I whispered.

"We are all girls, though. So maybe they will ignore us."

"But how do you know the Serbs are really going to do this? Blowing up a river! That's crazy. It's impossible to tell what's true around here. Maybe this is just another story to upset us."

"Well, it isn't. Listen, please don't tell Besim. I'm afraid he'll try to stop me. He just doesn't think the way we do, Adem. So don't tell him," she said. "Promise?"

"Okay," I said. But I shouldn't have. Here promises became fate. Here promises became chains that dragged you down.

Soon we'd be in the valley, making our way through the twisted streets of Prizren. I loved Prizren, too. It was full of old houses and mosques. Along the river in the evenings, everyone turned out to walk up and down the promenade in the cool night air that flowed down the steep mountainsides like streams. People would be there, walking with their friends and families, stopping at cafés, listening to music.

But now, with the Serb regime and the international sanctions, there were also other things going on at night in Prizren. There were border runners, smugglers, thieves, informers, police raids. The only way my mother would let us go to town was if we all promised to stay together the whole time.

"Come on," said Fatmira again, pulling me with her down the hill. "It's twenty after five."

"Let me see the poem," I said.

"No. It's nothing. It's short. Only a few lines. Do you know the myth of Demeter and Persephone?"

"From the Greeks?"

"Yes. Hades steals Persephone and takes her to the underworld. And Demeter, her mother, mourns her so fiercely that springtime never comes to the land. It's about that and how dry the year has been. The river is only a trickle right now. It's nearly disappeared."

My sister was very smart. I was proud of her for doing this. But, at the same time, I thought it was terribly stu-

pid, that our whole lives should be made of acts of op-
position every single day. What would this do for us after
years of resistance? Could it hurt us? Already I lay in bed
at night, worrying about my eyesight. Would I go blind
someday from the tear gas? My eyes still burned from
yesterday morning, and my vision was blurred. That was
because the tear gas made little holes like craters on the
surface of our eyes.

I turned to Pranvera and Besim. "Come on. Hurry, so
Fatmira won't be late."

We all started running. "Late for what?" Pranvera
called out.

But I pretended not to hear her.

We had a custom in Albanian culture called *besa*. It
meant that your honor depended on keeping your word.
But how could you keep your word in a place where
nothing was true and you didn't know what was real and
what was a lie? Whenever our Albanian culture teacher
stood in front of us to talk about *besa*, I wanted to ask
this question. I wanted to show her how wrong she was.
I wanted to punish her for saying this to us so often.

The other kids liked to hear about it. "Yes, yes," they
agreed. "That's how we Albanians are. We are proud, we
have solidarity."

Blah, blah, blah, I wanted to say. And sometimes I did.

Out in the school yard, the oldest boys frowned at me.
"You're a cynic, Adem. You have no hope. You'll get us
all in trouble one day. The Democratic Alliance is working hard for us every day."

"I want to have hope," I said. "But why should I hope if I don't know what's going on? I need the truth before I'm willing to hope. I need proof of what the Alliance has told us about things getting better. What's wrong with that?"

"There are reasons the Alliance doesn't tell us things," the kids said. "Important reasons."

"Oh, yeah? Like what?"

Then they got disgusted with me, and we chose sides for invisible soccer. We played it for a few minutes every day, our own little act of resistance. Because I was the goalie, many times I came in from recess with my knees raw and bleeding, but I didn't care.

The Serb kids would come out of their side of the school and stand around and watch us. We weren't supposed to talk to them or we could be punished, even expelled from school. Of course, the Serb kids knew this. They used to be our friends. But now they swore at us. They knew we played invisible soccer out of defiance.

"You Albanians are stupid, like cavemen. No, you're orangutans. You play soccer with no ball and don't even know the difference. How dumb can you get?"

We ignored them. If they threw rocks, we still ignored them—unless we got hit. Every day, we had to hide our anger and keep our faces and voices calm. Every day we had to destroy ourselves a little bit more, but when I made a spectacular dive for an invisible soccer ball, I felt a spark of pride. And I knew that, without guns, we were stronger than they were.

Suddenly Pranvera tugged on my hand and pulled me through the crowd. She had spotted a cart selling doughnuts.

"I have money," she said. "Please, Adem."

She opened her hand and showed me one coin.

"Okay," I said. "Let's see how much they cost."

We walked over to the cart. Each doughnut sat in a little crinkled cup of white paper. Stuck into the doughnut with a toothpick was a tiny Serb flag. They were Serb doughnuts. We shouldn't buy them. But I could see that Pranvera liked the little flag. It was like a toy flag for a dollhouse.

"Please?" she asked again. She touched one of the little flags with her finger.

I looked around for Besim. He had wandered away with some friends. I was about to say yes when Fatmira came and snatched her away. "We don't have time for that now," she said. "After I read my poem, we'll get some ice cream from the Albanian shop on the other side of the river."

Just then Besim reappeared. He sensed the tension in Fatmira and me. "What's going on?" he asked.

Fatmira turned away and pretended she hadn't heard. It was nearly six o'clock.

"Nothing," I mumbled, but I could feel the excitement running through the crowd of Albanians along the riverbank as the time came near. This was too dangerous, I thought. I'd better let Besim decide what to do.

But the clock in the tower near the old mosque was

striking six, and already the five high-school girls had walked to the center of the bridges as planned.

The girl lowest down the river read her poem first. Fatmira was second to last. All the Albanians who were out walking stopped along the promenade to listen in silence. We had been staging peaceful protests for years, so people knew at once what to do. No one needed to tell us how or when to support one another.

After the first poem, the crowd grew larger. Everyone began to chant "De-moc-ra-cy," over and over again. A flare of energy flowed through the crowd. I looked around excitedly. There was no way the Serbs could ignore us if we kept this up. Maybe we could get our schoolbooks back this year.

Besim and I stood at the edge of the dried-up river, while, on the fourth bridge, Fatmira waited for her turn to read. Special police in their blue uniforms and boots were now running toward the river, pushing people with their truncheons and plastic shields to make them disperse. As soon as the police cleared one group away, a new group of Albanians chanting for democracy came to take their place. A jeep drove along the promenade. A Serb policeman with a bullhorn stood in the front seat. He ordered us to leave the area at once or they would open fire.

I paid no attention. I thought he meant they'd shoot tear gas. Tear gas twice in one week? Why not? If Fatmira could take it, I could, too.

Besim spoke. "Let's not do this," he said. "I'm going to get her. It's not worth it."

The police were using clubs now to disperse us. There was a lot of shouting behind me and a scream. Suddenly gunfire rang out from the jeep. They were shooting randomly over my head across the river. I heard two bursts of rapid machine-gun fire of about twenty seconds each.

I started running across the bridge. "Fatmira, get down! Get down!" I screamed.

But it was too late. She had already fallen. I threw myself on her and shook her to try to rouse her, but she wouldn't wake up. Big hands pried me off her body. From her hand I quickly took the folded piece of paper and slipped it into my pocket. I didn't want the Serb police to find the poem on her.

As the police pulled me away, I could see blood and a black bullet hole burned through her denim jacket in the middle of her back. Someone had turned her over. Her face was white. Blood trickled from the corner of her mouth.

I was screaming her name and wouldn't stop. The police brushed me aside and loaded her into their jeep. I grabbed on to the door handle and tried to climb in, too. "Let me go with you!" I screamed. "Don't take her away. I can make her better."

The police pushed me away and quickly drove through the crowd.

"Where is she going?" I cried over and over again.

An old Albanian woman in a traditional black dress came and took my arm. "Calm down, it's all right," she said. "They've taken her to the hospital. It's not far. You can find her there."

"Leave me alone," I yelled, wrenching my arm from her grasp.

Pranvera pushed her way through the crowd and clung to my waist. We ran with Besim to the hospital, but they wouldn't let us see her. We stood in the entrance until two officials came from the Democratic Alliance. They weren't allowed in either.

"She's in the operating room," the Serb doctors said. "Come back tomorrow. You can see her tomorrow."

FOUR

All night, my parents sat at the kitchen table waiting for enough morning light to travel into town. But they never left. In the light of a pale, gray dawn, the police brought Fatmira's body to our house. The side of her face was covered with dried blood. The blood had dried in her hair. She was dirty and her jacket was torn. There had been no operation.

The police handed her body to my father, who took her in his arms, staggering with her weight. In the doorway, he turned around to show us. We all stood in the hall. His mouth had dropped open. Fatmira's head fell back. Her throat looked long and arched. My mother began to wail and shriek and tear wildly at her clothes. My grandmother restrained her as best she could. Pranvera ran for my uncle to help us.

My mother's family came that afternoon from Pristina. The next day, Fatmira's body had been cleaned and made ready for burial. She lay on the boards of the Muslim coffin. The open top was covered by the red Albanian flag with its black double-headed eagle.

While my aunts and grandmothers and mother prepared her body, one of them said, "She was the bravest girl who ever lived. She was a heroine for Kosovo."

She had been beautiful, with long, dark brown hair, nearly black, and deep, dark eyes. She had laughed a lot. Now, as she lay on the boards, her top lip was drawn back so that her teeth showed. She might have been laughing if she were alive.

I kept away from the coffin and the wailing, going outside even in the drizzle. I walked with my cow, stroking her smooth brown side, scratching behind her ears with a stick. She loved that. Mostly we stayed under the apple trees just behind the house because it was raining. It was one of the few times it had rained since spring.

Maybe that was why the special police were not prepared for the thousands who came to Fatmira's funeral. Albanian people came from all over the province of Kosovo to her funeral in our little village. Many of them came during the night, in the drizzle and fog, and many more came at dawn.

No one spoke. People quietly lined the dirt lane to our house. They stood silently in the ditches with their funeral wreaths, a wreath for everyone who had been killed so far, and large wreaths for the other eleven children who had been shot in Prizren. The line stretched for miles on both sides of the road.

Later I hated all those people for coming.

If only no one had come.

My father and Besim had dug her grave in our corn-field, close to the side of the road, so that, later, people could find it easily. But I refused to help them. I sat in my parents' bedroom and cried. The grave was a stupid little hole. Behind it rose the sharp mountains of Albania, the secret paths to freedom beyond the border.

When the time came, I helped Papa, Besim, and Uncle Sal lead the procession and carry the open coffin to the grave past the crowds of people mourning Fatmira. We lowered her body into the dirt hole and covered her over. That was the worst part. The wet lumps of dirt felt heavy and dead. I couldn't stand it. I couldn't stand leaving her there, dwarfed by the base of the mountain.

Then came the speeches. Our political leaders got up on a little platform to speak into a microphone. The microphone was wired to a speaker on the roof of their car. They wore suits and ties, the shoulders of their jackets darkened with rain. Their wet hair separated into thick strands that clung to their heads.

"Fatmira will not be forgotten," one said. "We must keep on our course of peaceful resistance and international diplomacy in Sweden, Switzerland, the United States. We must stay calm and show the Serbs our unity. Fatmira was a courageous girl. She is the daughter of us all."

That, I knew, was a lie. I clenched my fists and dug my fingernails into my palms. I wanted my hands to bleed, but they wouldn't. How dare they talk about my sister? They didn't even know her. Now they acted as if she were their own daughter, their own sister. They would force her to live on and on, and our family would become the family of Fatmira.

During the speeches, Serb police and tanks came slowly up the long hill road from Prizren to our little village, shooting canisters of tear gas into the crowd. And for once I was glad. Because of the tear gas and the rain, everyone soon left. It was over, I told myself. My life would go on as it had before.

I wanted to get used to Fatmira being dead. I wanted to be like other kids again, but it wouldn't happen that way. Fatmira meant "good luck." But whatever good luck my family had once had, it was now gone forever.

Every day, right through September, people came to Fatmira's grave and left flowers. I was sick of flowers. Flowers once picked were weak. Without soil, without water, they quickly wilted in the hot sun. Then my mother made me go and clean them off the grave. Dahlias dropped a million petals shaped like tiny red swords in the grass. I had to pick them up.

Every day now, soldiers stood in our road. Sometimes they let everyone come. Sometimes they stopped people, demanded their identification cards, and forced them to leave. Pranvera and I watched from the window. There was nearly always an armored vehicle parked in front of our house. When we went out, we went only as far as the field out back.

At first, I kept thinking Fatmira was in the house. It seemed as if she were about to come into the room. I heard her voice, and my heart fluttered up like a startled bird, until I realized once more that she was dead and lying under a pile of dirt.

But maybe I was the one who had turned into a ghost. I stopped speaking to everyone except Pranvera, whom in my anger I bossed around and yelled at whenever I got the chance.

I started spending as much time as Besim did in the cement-walled bathroom behind the kitchen. It was not heated and there was no toilet, just a hole to stand over, and a sink. But on the back of the door there was a mirror. It was covered over with my father's farm clothes and a big, worn-out towel that he used when he came in from the field. I pushed aside the dirty towel and stared at myself. What had I done? Had I caused my sister's death by not telling her secret? How could I go on like this? How could my family go on with my mother crying in silence as she and my grandmother served us men supper?

I couldn't eat. It started the first night after the funeral, when we had mutton. It had been cooked the day before, then kept in the cold oven overnight. My mother brought it to the table already cut into big, dry chunks of meat and bone. Pranvera served us bread and Coke and bitter lettuce with chopped scallions. My mother placed a dry chunk of meat on each plate. The smell of the sheep fat made me gag.

"Eat up," my father said, pointing his knife at my plate. He ate ravenously.

I couldn't swallow. Even the Coke tasted bad to me, strange and metallic, instead of sweet. The tears ran down my mother's face. Every so often, she blew her nose. Her nostrils were red and sore. How could her body make so many tears?

My grandfather leaned toward me. "Don't let the Serbs take your appetite as well," he whispered.

Jealous of the attention I was getting, Besim said, "Give me your meat, then."

I slid the chunk of mutton onto his plate. He took the lettuce, too.

Every day after that, I continued to have trouble swallowing. Food seemed to get stuck in my throat. I was becoming thinner. I already knew I had stopped growing. When I looked in the mirror, my head, nose, and ears looked big, almost man-sized, but my shoulders were narrow and shrunken. My arms and legs had grown long—or started to—but my body had stopped right where it was.

I looked deformed. I was a freak. As I stared at the bathroom mirror, I whispered the harshest names I could think of to punish myself for what I had done.

My mother knew I was in there. She could hear the sound of my father's clothes being pushed aside. One night, after ten or fifteen minutes, she burst through the door to scold me. "Come on, come on. You shouldn't do this." Then she rubbed my shoulders vigorously, as though that would force energy back into my body. "Take a walk. Get some fresh air, okay?"

I wandered outside and down the street to the village park. I could see a group of Serb boys playing keep-away down there, but I pretended· to myself that they were invisible. They could not affect me.

And so I kept walking. I saw that Milos was with them. As I got nearer, one of them yelled out, "Go back to Albania where you belong." It was because of Fatmira that they were yelling at me. Their parents had probably told them that I was a troublemaker.

"Serbia is for Serbs!" another yelled.

I ducked my head away so they couldn't see that my eyes were full of tears.

"Shut up, you two," Milos yelled at them.

He grabbed the ball and ran toward me. He knew me well enough to know I was crying. For a crazy moment, I thought that somehow we could become friends again.

He began walking with me. We didn't speak at first. I kicked at some loose rocks in the road.

Finally he said, "I'm sorry about your sister."

I nodded.

Then he burst out, "But the funeral, Adem. Why do you people do that?"

I stopped and looked at him. I didn't know what he meant. "Do what?" I asked.

"Why do you always have those big demonstrations? Bosnia and Croatia have already torn Yugoslavia apart. Do you think our army can sit back and watch demonstrations like that and do nothing? We have to keep order in Kosovo, can't you see that?"

"Not by killing, not by violence," I said.

"But we have to use force. You understand nothing else. You're trying to drive us out of our sacred heartland, the home of the Serbian people."

"No we're not. That's not true!"

"Yes it is," said Milos. "You've elected a government full of Albanian traitors to overthrow us. That was illegal. That was why our President had to send in tanks. As long as you don't cooperate, there's going to be trouble," Milos said earnestly. "You're bringing it on yourselves. Please, Adem. You must listen."

I couldn't speak. I could only stare at him. None of what he said was true at all, but he so clearly believed it. The distance between us was huge. I didn't know what to say. Choking back tears, I shook my head and walked away. I walked on to a small kiosk that sold candy and soda, and bought a pack of gum. I unwrapped the package slowly as I started back up the hill to our house so I would look normal, like a kid buying gum, nothing more than that.

When I got home, I found Besim watching TV. I sat down next to him on the sofa. I told him what had happened with me and Milos. "He really believes that we want to destroy Serbia," I said.

Besim shrugged. "What do you expect? The Serbs are liars, that's all."

He got up to change the station. I lay down on the other sofa and put the pillow over my head. I thought I would miss Fatmira forever.

FIVE

It was early October now, one month since the funeral. In America, they had a scary holiday called Halloween. Besim brought home some black-market videos of scary movies, which he had copied for the VCR. We watched them over and over again. I loved the gore, the violence, the dead bodies and green fingernails. I loved the deformities—hunchbacks and werewolves. Vampires. Howling dogs.

"Stop watching this, you two," my mother said. "We have chores to do if nothing else. You haven't made the mounds for the potatoes. We need three of them. And what about the peppers?"

When we ignored her, she stood in front of the set.

"No more. You want to go hungry this winter? Do you?"

My mother would nag us nonstop, but she wouldn't

turn off the set because Besim and I were men. Albanian boys were lucky. I was glad I wasn't a girl.

She handed me a cardboard box. I put it over my head and sat looking at the TV through the slits.

"You're driving me mad!" she finally shouted. "Don't you think I'm filled with sorrow and grief, Adem? Do you think it's only you who feels these things?"

Everyone, even Fatmira, had accused me of this, of being selfish. But I had never meant to be.

My mother started to cry. I felt bad then, and went out and worked hard to fill the box with red and yellow peppers. As I stooped over the slender pepper plants, I thought about Fatmira helping the younger children the day we'd been teargassed. When I'd wanted to jump up and run back to the school, she'd told me that that might cause the teachers to be beaten even more. I'd never thought of that. Maybe Mama and Fatmira were right, then. But what could I do to change? I filled the box until it was piled high with peppers. Everyone had respected Fatmira; everyone thought that one day she would be a leader.

"Well, look who's turned into a farmer!" my Uncle Sal shouted at me from the farm wagon. Our old horse was pulling the wagon toward the house.

He and my father were bringing in loads of potatoes, which we would shovel into long mounds of dirt for winter storage. They would sprout that way and be ready to plant in the spring. I watched them come across the field. I saw that my father's shoulders were stooped with tiredness. I vowed that tomorrow I would dig the dirt mounds to keep the potatoes safe from frost, and I wouldn't even worry about whether Besim was helping or not. I had never realized until now how much farmwork Fatmira had done. Without her, shoveling the mounds would be pure drudgery. But we had to get the vegetables in before a hard frost or they would rot.

I carried the box of peppers into the kitchen to show my mother. She was rolling out the paper-thin dough needed to make *burek*. She rolled it with a broomstick on the kitchen table. Her hands were dusted white with flour, so I couldn't give her the box. I stood next to her and waited. She seemed lost in thought, rolling out the crust and then flipping it over and doing it again. Little balls of white dough sat on a plate, awaiting their turn to be flattened. Suddenly she noticed me still holding the peppers.

"Adem!" she cried. "Oh, thank you." She wiped her floury hands, then took my face and gave me a big kiss on the cheek.

I went out and set the box of peppers by the back door.

The special police came at two o'clock in the morning. I was sleeping on a living room sofa, a light, hazy doze during which I turned restlessly back and forth. Besim slept soundly on the other sofa, lying on his back, snoring.

When the jeeps pulled up, I was already awake, as though this were what I had been waiting for. Finally, I thought, the police had come for me. The house was cold at night in early October. We were high up near the mountains. My feet were freezing on the marble-tiled floor. My white flannel pajamas were way too small. My legs stuck out at the bottom like a scarecrow's.

I opened the front door just as they were about to bang on it.

That startled them, and at first they laughed. Then the leader said in Serbian, "Turn on the lights."

We all knew the Serb language very well, but none of them ever learned to speak Albanian. They couldn't understand us.

I flicked the switch, but the room stayed dark. No electricity. The leader swore and pulled out a big flashlight.

"Papa, Papa!" I shouted as they pushed past me.

Besim and Papa slept alike—like stones. My mother woke up first and hurried down the stairs. The six policemen were inside now. One of them prodded Besim awake with his rifle. When Besim opened his eyes and saw a rifle being poked into his ribs, he screamed in terror. The policemen laughed and pulled him roughly to his feet, shining the beams from their flashlights in his eyes.

"Where are the weapons you're keeping in here?" they shouted at him. I thought maybe they had come to take him for the Serb army.

Besim's hair stuck up like a rooster's. He stared at them without speaking. They began to turn the living room upside down. My father came downstairs and my grandparents came from their apartment. The police knocked over the tables, threw the paintings on the floor, and shattered my mother's fancy Turkish coffee cups, their green rims decorated with arabesque designs in gold. They dumped all our boxes of photographs on the floor and trampled on them. One policeman crouched down and tried to set them on fire with a match. They ripped down my mother's red velvet curtains while she pleaded with them not to.

We watched them destroy our kitchen, dumping out our flour and salt. Would we keep guns in the flour?

"Please," said my father. "We have no weapons. None at all."

"Confess!" one said and struck him across the face. My father stayed silent.

They went upstairs. We could hear them rampaging from room to room, pulling closets apart, dumping out our clothes, knocking over beds and chairs. When they came down again, they were laughing and had taken out their truncheons. Two grabbed my father, one by each arm. They pulled his arms behind him so that he hung forward between them, almost suspended. They knew that the worst humiliation for an Albanian man was to destroy his honor in front of his family. My mother picked up Halil and pressed his face against her shoulder so he wouldn't see.

They prodded us with their rifles and made Besim, Pranvera, me, and our mother and grandparents line up in the hall while they held my father. They kicked him in the groin, shouting, "No more children, you animal!"

My father groaned and bent double from the blows, but for our sake he tried not to cry out. None of us moved or made a sound, not even Halil. They took their clubs and beat him on the back and sides, then in the face. We hoped that if we all stayed quiet, they wouldn't take him away. So we made no move to stop them.

"Who organized the funeral? Who is your leader?"

"I don't know!" my father cried. "No one organized it. People just came."

"Liar! Tell us who organized it. We want names."

"I don't know!"

They beat him some more about the face and head. Blood streamed from his nose. Already one side of his face had begun to swell. Then one policeman took his club and beat him on the ear. My father staggered, but he could not fall because they held him. After ten minutes, they stopped, out of breath. My father was unconscious, but we could hear his breath coming in raspy gasps. Maybe his ribs were broken. They must be.

In anguish and fear, I had urinated into my pajamas. I saw that Besim had, too. I felt full of shame and didn't want the policemen to know.

They dragged my father to the door. Two of them took him away.

"Wait! Wait! Where are you taking him?" my mother cried, running to the doorstep. "He needs a doctor!"

They didn't answer. One of them, a tall one, turned and jabbed his rifle between her legs.

"No more Albanian children," he said. "You should learn to control yourself."

Then they shoved our father into the jeep and left. We weren't sure where they would take him. We turned and looked at our house. The walls were still standing, it's true, but our house was destroyed.

"Mama," I whispered, "let's leave. Please, let's go away from here."

If they had come once, they would come again. That was the pattern. We knew many people this had happened to for one reason or another. But she didn't hear me.

My mother and grandfather went into Prizren the next day to see if they could find my father. It was important to let the police know that we were looking for him. But they would tell her nothing. She brought an Albanian doctor later in the afternoon and demanded that he be allowed to examine my father, but they wouldn't agree to that.

That night two Democratic Alliance leaders came from the Prizren office to talk to us, including Dr. Dedusha, who was head of the Prizren Alliance. They counseled my mother to be calm. They would help her find my father. They photographed the damage to the house and had my mother describe in detail what had happened. This they would keep in the records of human rights violations.

Pranvera, Besim, and I sat politely and quietly in a row on one of the sofas while they talked with my mother and grandfather for a long time. My grandmother served them little glasses of raki, a brandy, and cookies neatly arranged on a plate. I stared at the circular pattern of the cookies. How ridiculous people were—at once arranging cookies that would be eaten and disappear, while they also sought to destroy each other with hatred. It seemed so odd that I was still alive and Fatmira wasn't, and that my father had been imprisoned when he had done nothing wrong. None of it made sense.

After they left, my mother said, "They say they'll try to help, but who knows? We're only village people, farmers, not doctors or lawyers. Adem, go get Avni's father for me."

I pulled on my sneakers and ran up the lane to Avni's small stone house. The goats that rambled freely through the rocks in the front yard were taking shelter for the night under rusted pieces of sheet metal leaning against the wall. I nearly stepped on a roosting hen as I banged on the door.

"Avni! Avni!"

Avni and his mother opened the door, peering out suspiciously to see who was there. Avni's mother was enormous. I couldn't understand this—her children were so thin. She was wheezing and taking short little breaths.

"Good evening," I said politely. "My mother needs to talk with your husband."

"What for?" she asked.

"A business deal."

She didn't answer. Still, she went off to get him, while Avni leaned against the doorway and stared at me. Behind him in the kitchen, two little children looked at me from under their matted, tangled hair.

Avni's father was named Driton, which meant "light." It was our custom to give children names like that. Pranvera meant "spring." Besim meant "honor." I was named after an Albanian author, Adem Demaqi, who had been imprisoned for writing about democracy. He had been a prisoner of conscience for twenty-seven years. Now he was part of the Democratic Alliance.

Driton came to the door wearing a worn gray sports coat, a mustard-colored shirt, and torn dark pants. I was wearing my winter jacket and had had to keep my hands in my pockets all the way up. I worried that he would be cold on the walk down the hill to our house.

"Should you get a coat?" I asked.

"No. I'll be fine," he said. "Come on."

He strode ahead of me, and when he got to our house, he went inside without knocking. My mother and grand-father met him at the doorway, and then they quickly shooed me out of the room. What on earth could they want from him? I supposed it was possible that, for money from us, he would find out where my father was being held. I sat at the top of the stairs and waited.

At first their voices were loud, arguing back and forth. I heard him say that it was too dangerous for him to get involved in this. Then my grandfather listed all the times we had helped his family in the past. Often, at the end of the day, my grandmother had given one of us a loaf of bread to take up to their house. We had kept them from starving, my grandfather said. That made Driton fall quiet. He agreed to help us if he could.

What if my father never came home again? Why had I let Fatmira go to read her poem? How could a hand-ful of unspoken words have hurt our family so much and changed our lives forever?

I kept the poem in my pocket always. I took it out, as

I had a thousand times already. I didn't really understand all of it, but I was sure that somehow it held a clue to the silent mysteries that were swirling around me.

Children, Be Still

by Fatmira Hoti

Amid black-faced flowers, our
river runs dry. The stones lie like
clattering bones in their bed. Enemy
gunfire rattles down cobbled streets.
We can be stilled, but we are
still children, and each spring
we will reappear,
running across the old bridges,
with many voices,
shouting and laughing
in the new rain.

If only I knew what she had meant, then maybe I could do something. All I understood was that she had tried to speak out. But we were supposed to keep silent, to "be still." Not only the Serbs, but also the Democratic Alliance insisted on this silence. The leaders of the Alliance alone were supposed to speak about politics so that we could show the world our unity. With their poems, Fatmira and the other girls had broken that rule.

Fatmira had been the smart one in the family. My father had told everyone that when she turned eighteen, she would go to the university at Pristina—until the

Serbs closed it to Albanians. Then he bragged that one day he would take her across the mountains to freedom, and that one day she would come back home and save us all. She had always been destined for this.

I couldn't wait for Driton to leave. I wanted to go downstairs so I could fall asleep instantly and never wake up.

SIX

Every day for five days, my mother went to the police station. Every day they told her the same thing: they didn't know where my father was. It was possible that he was already dead, they suggested. He could die of a fractured skull or internal bleeding. It happened.

The weather turned bitterly cold for October while my father was gone. Besim and I spent six hours a day cutting firewood and stacking it beside the back door. We didn't go to school. The fifth morning, there was even a snow flurry. My mother and Pranvera had cleaned most of the house by then. I took ripped clothing, a shattered table, and torn-up books and burned them in the garbage heap past the apple trees. The fire roared and crackled. Ashes rose from the fire, mixing with the big flakes that were floating slowly down. From underneath, both the ashes and the snow looked pale gray. I couldn't tell one from the other.

Pranvera brought out a plastic shopping bag filled with ripped and stained photographs that my mother wanted me to burn. I tossed the whole pile on the fire. At first, because they settled on the flames in a flat disk, they nearly smothered that section of the fire. Smoke encircled them, and the edges began to curl and turn brown.

I poked at the photos with my stick. Then I noticed one of Fatmira from several years ago. We had gone to Montenegro, to the beach, during a time before the embargo, when we still had gasoline and were allowed to travel. She had her head tilted to one side and she was laughing. I remembered that day—how we had flung ourselves wildly into the water for hours, then lay on the warm sand. It had been a day of happiness, a day without fear. I reached into the fire and grabbed the photo and shoved it in my pocket. Then I watched the rest of the pictures catch fire and burn.

In a way, I liked burning our things. Without telling my mother, I brought my pajamas out and burned them, too. From now on, I would sleep in my clothes.

The flames warmed my face. I could feel my own skin clearly separating me from the surrounding air and smoke, containing me in a life no one else would ever quite know. I stood by the fire a long time, feeling this sense that I was both separate and alive, my heart pounding in my chest. It was a feeling I wanted to share with Fatmira. I knew she would have understood.

———

That night, after supper, Avni's father came back to the house. When I opened the door, he pushed past me, barely saying hello, and hurried for a place by the heater. He started to speak, but my grandfather gestured for Pranvera to bring a glass of raki for each of them. One night he was giving raki to Dr. Dedusha, the next night to an informer. Our life was insane.

Raki was a clear fruit brandy that tasted like liquid fire. Every fall, my grandfather made some from the grapes we grew in the courtyard. It tasted awful. They were crazy to drink that stuff. It was traditional, my father said. Who cared? Besim and I sat on one of the sofas at the side of the room and were quiet. That was traditional, too.

Driton cleared his throat. "Tomorrow, at four, at the back door to the police station, he'll be released. But no crowds, you must promise me. No demonstrations. The paperwork to release him has already been completed. And you'd better bring a car. He's very weak."

"Have you seen him?" cried my mother.

Driton nodded.

"How bad is he?" she asked.

Driton hesitated. Then he said to her, "He is getting better now."

"But how bad was it?" she insisted.

"I—I've seen worse." Driton downed his raki and coughed. "Maybe this will be the end of the trouble for you."

"Did the police say that?" she asked quickly.

"No," he said. "They guarantee nothing."

"They don't know what they're doing," my grandfather said bitterly. "It is all completely by whim. One day this, one day that. It's accidental, what happens to us. We don't matter at all, not even enough for them to take the trouble to plan for us what will happen. The Nazis were like that."

My mother got up and left the room without saying anything. But I knew she went to get money, which was hidden upstairs. She didn't want Driton to know where we kept it. When the special police were short of cash, they stopped by people's homes and took whatever money they could find. Driton could easily have made a little extra cash by telling them where our money box was.

My mother came back and handed him the cash and he counted it. Then he got up. My grandmother rose as well and began to collect the tiny raki glasses on the silver tray.

"Thank you," Driton said. "Good night."

"With money and brandy, his manners have returned," my grandmother murmured on her way to the kitchen.

The next day, the Democratic Alliance helped my mother get a car and a doctor to drive my father home. We stood waiting outside the house for two hours, worrying that maybe something had gone wrong.

Little Halil was fussy and anxious. First I held him, then Pranvera did, but he wouldn't stop squirming and crying. Finally my grandmother had to take him inside.

Around six o'clock, other people from the village began to wait by our house as well. Everyone wanted to see how badly my father had been beaten and tortured. Whether Serb or Albanian, they came out of curiosity. I was furious to see them all standing there.

The car pulled up to our house. Everyone stood back. My mother and the doctor got out, supporting my father between them, and led him into the house. Pranvera and I ran inside after them and slammed the door. The driver waited outside in the car so that he could take the doctor back to Prizren later.

They laid my father on a sofa in the living room. Pranvera and I had turned on the heater right after my mother left for town so the room would be warm. I couldn't believe how swollen one side of his face still was. It looked like an inflated ball, blue and green instead of flesh-colored. One of his ears was badly swollen, and the doctor said he had no hearing on that side. His front teeth had been knocked out, and his top lip was split wide open and covered with dried blood. He smelled of musty, sour sweat and urine.

But the bad part was that he didn't seem to see us. He didn't seem to know he was home.

"We rescued you, Papa," Pranvera said. But he didn't move or turn his head.

"Welcome home, Papa," I said. "We turned on the heater for you." But it didn't matter if he was warm. He no longer cared.

SEVEN

In part of our house, a room at the front, my grandmother kept a little shop that sold bread, eggs, yogurt, and candy. It was hard to tell the shop was there at all. The only sign was the faded lettering on an old piece of plywood that leaned against the cement-block wall. The sign said BUKE, which meant "bread." Sometimes she sold Coke, too.

Everyone grew peppers, scallions, bitter lettuce, and potatoes, just as we did. But, in the mornings, people came to my grandmother's shop for their bread and eggs. The bread was baked very early by women in the village and then sold for a pittance. Still, it helped to keep us from starving. Even if you had relatives in America trying to send you money, sometimes months passed with no word. As for our jobs and stores, the laws had been changed. We could own nothing now. The Serbs had laid claim to all our jobs, land, houses, schools, property—everything.

The Serbs wanted to take over Kosovo. Only 20 percent of the Albanians could stay. But we were now nearly 90 percent of the population. Where could two million of us go? We had no cars, no money, no passport visas, and the United Nations refugee camps were far away in Croatia and Germany. Besides, people had to spend years in those overcrowded camps. The living conditions were terrible, and families were split up for no reason.

Here, the rocks and trees were ours. The mines and the vineyards. The cornfields and the little red foxes that ran under the stars. We lived here. That was the problem. And the Serbs said we were different from them. That was worse. They called us animals. But no animals I'd ever seen would hurt one another the way people did.

Through October, November, and into December, my father sat in the front room. He rarely spoke. The swelling in his cheek went down. An Albanian dentist came and took out his broken teeth. But now his mouth looked oddly soft and dented in, like dough or a shriveled apple. Sometimes he got up and went and stood under the apple trees without his coat. Although his ear looked normal again, the hearing in it never returned.

Now that it was December, it was dark in the afternoons. We still stayed home from school because there was no electricity or heat there. The Serbs turned it off so we couldn't study.

My father sat all morning staring at the TV. Serb news

shows, mostly. It didn't matter to him what he watched. In the afternoon, he slept. Then, if there was electricity, he watched the evening news. It was all nationalist propaganda from Belgrade, but he watched it anyway. Otherwise he sat in the kitchen by the woodstove in the dark.

One night, on Serb TV news from Belgrade, the weatherman was talking about the severe drought we were having. It was terrible everywhere, especially in Vojvodina, in the north, near Hungary. But I didn't believe it could be worse there than here. They never mentioned the word "Kosovo" on TV because they wanted the Serb people to forget about us. They wanted the world to forget about us.

The weatherman said the severe drought had been caused by the American President. He had sent poisoned clouds to Serbia because he hated the Slavic people.

Pranvera was watching TV with us. "If their President sent poison," she said happily, "then maybe he will send the tanks next!"

According to the next news segment, the Bosnian Muslims were inhuman and needed to be destroyed. They had fed Serb babies to the zoo animals in Sarajevo.

I clapped my hands over my ears and screamed. What madness! I got up and turned off the TV.

"Turn it on!" shouted my grandfather from his chair. "I want to hear the lies."

He was my grandfather, so I had to do what he said, but I kept my hands over my ears and refused to listen.

Through it all, my father didn't speak. After the news,

he went out front and stood in the road, looking up at the mountains rising to the west. If Uncle Sal had time, he came in the afternoon and evening and sat next to him, smoking cigarettes. My father started smoking, too.

I watched out the window. What had they done to him in the jail? Where had he gone?

We all took too many naps. One afternoon, my mother shook me awake.

"That's it," she said. "No more sleeping. We're going to have a party."

I sat up, groggy and confused about what day it was.

"Party?" I echoed.

"We'll have an extra-big New Year's party this year. It will be a party of hope that our worst times are over," she said. All my nearby cousins and relatives would come from the village and from Pristina. "We'll have presents and special food and dancing all night. It'll be just like the old days."

I thought she was crazy at first, and I helped out reluctantly. Unfortunately, the first thing she wanted me to do was clean. I complained a lot about having to help with the housework, but actually it felt good to have things to do. As I dragged one of the heavy carpets outdoors to beat the dust from it, I could see that she was forcing herself to be cheerful for our sake, mine and Pranvera's and Halil's. I realized that my mother was strong, that she was the one who would somehow get us through these bad times and keep our spirits alive.

"Adem, you beat those rugs with a broom until not a speck of dust is left," she called out the door.

The carpets were big and heavy, with Turkish designs on them. When I was a baby, my mother and father had traveled to Turkey once to get them. Carpets were very cheap in Istanbul.

My mother played tapes of Albanian folksongs while we cleaned. But no matter how lively the beat was, the songs all sounded sad to me. Always people were being separated from one another, being torn apart. Some of the songs were centuries old, but they were all about the same thing: losing your family. It seemed that Albanian families were destined to be forced apart. I gritted my teeth as I beat the rugs. Could that happen to us?

After we'd cleaned the entire house, my mother retreated into the kitchen. She and my grandmother baked a dough pie called *flie*. My grandmother cooked it outside in a wide pan over a charcoal fire. It took hours to make. The truth was, nobody liked it very much except for my grandfather, but we all had to pretend we did. My mother wrapped jars of pickled peppers and spicy relishes as presents for all our cousins. I stopped watching TV with my grandfather and father and stayed in the kitchen.

On the day before New Year's Eve, my mother sent me and Pranvera out for a little evergreen tree. I carried the hatchet. We wandered up the lane to the mountain path.

"Where are we going to find a tree?" I asked Pranvera, not expecting an answer. So many had been cut down by now, it wouldn't be easy.

It was cold, and I hadn't brought any mittens. We

didn't have boots either, and there was an inch or two of slippery snow on the ground. We followed a narrow gully as it twisted its way along the side of the mountain.

Eventually, after half an hour's walk, we found a little tree. It seemed a shame to cut it down.

Pranvera sat on a rock and stared at it. I could see that she felt bad about cutting it, too. But at home we had a string of colored tinsel and paper chains to put on it, and the party was tomorrow.

Finally she said, "Adem, we have to have it for the party."

So I chopped into the soft, wet pinewood with the hatchet, and between us we started to drag it home.

The sun set behind the western mountains around three, making the afternoons in December and early January long and dismal. It had been a cloudy day with snow flurries, so it was very dark. We looked like two shadows stumbling on the dirt lane, dragging the tree.

We came to Fatmira's grave. My mother had put several candles around the burial mound. Pranvera and I stopped and looked at the mound of dirt. Then we dragged the tree onto her grave and sat down for a moment.

I glanced at my younger sister, and for the first time I saw her clearly. Usually I ignored her or raced her or waited for her, or took out my frustration on her, but somehow I'd never thought of her as a separate person. She'd been just a part of my family scene. And I thought that maybe one day she would travel far away from me and I from her, and all the hundreds of years of our traditional Albanian family would come to an end.

"Do you miss Fatmira?" I asked.

She nodded. Then my heart started pounding. I would tell my secret to Pranvera. She would understand that what I'd done was only a mistake, that I would never have caused Fatmira any harm. I'd tell her right now.

"Come on," Pranvera said. "It's getting cold." She started to get up.

"No, wait!" And then I knew that I wouldn't say anything to her. She was only a child; how could I expect her to understand? I realized at that point that I would have to tell my mother. She was the only one who could face the truth.

"What?" Pranvera asked impatiently. "Come on, Adem. I'm freezing."

I stood up. Someone was coming down the lane, heavily bundled in a winter jacket. We both watched the figure walking and sliding on ice patches as it approached us. The darkness of the mountains loomed behind us. I let out a big sigh.

The person walking toward us was Milos, bundled up in coat and gloves. He kept his head ducked down low into his scarf as he walked past Fatmira's grave.

"Hi," I said. But he didn't answer.

Pranvera and I pulled the tree to the house. As we dragged it over the doorstep, it brought a little puff of fresh mountain air inside. We dusted off the snow. When the tree had dried, we decorated it with tinsel and ornaments and put it in the living room. Even my father noticed it.

And the next day—with all our cousins, aunts, and

uncles—was a day filled with Albanian food and music and dancing until four o'clock in the morning. We toasted my sister's memory, and my mother cried, but it felt good to have the family all together. It was a night without fear. It was nearly dawn when I went to bed. Just before I went to sleep, I vowed that I would tell my mother my secret.

EIGHT

But I didn't. Not at first. And somehow most of the winter passed. I don't remember much of it. We all slept a lot, watched movies when Besim could find some, or went outside and wandered around just to get out of the house. School reopened at the end of February.

Gradually the sun stayed longer above our roof. By March, the birds were returning from Africa. In front of the house, a thin row of daffodil stalks had come up, but the flower buds stayed tightly closed. Out in the apple trees, the branches filled with flocks of black crows. They were the noisy ones that screeched for hours—caw, caw, caw—and drove you crazy.

After the crows returned, soldiers came to our house.

It was late afternoon. We had all been home from school for several hours. The bread and eggs had been sold for the day when the soldiers entered my grand-mother's little shop. Three of them came inside. There were six more outside in a second jeep. Each opened a Coke and drank it while I watched from the doorway. I felt that I should stop them, but I also knew they wanted me to try. So I didn't.

My grandmother always wore a kerchief over her hair, a white apron, and thick black wool leggings under her skirt. She was very short—nowhere near five feet tall—but that didn't stop her.

"Pay me for the Cokes!" she said, holding out her palm and shouting at them loudly in Albanian as though they were deaf.

They laughed and laid their automatic rifles on the counter.

"Give us your money box," the tall one said. He reached under the counter, took her box of money, and emptied the coins into the other soldiers' cupped palms. Then they led her to the door and pushed her out.

"Go on, old woman," said another soldier in Serb. "We're taking possession of the store now. We need to keep some soldiers closer to the village center to keep an eye on you troublemakers. We'll be living right next door to you. Won't that be nice?"

They pushed us both out and slammed the door. I stood in the road, stunned. There would be only a cement wall separating us from them. We had to be treated this way because we had disrupted the unity of Serbia. We were lucky to be alive, that was what they said. My grandmother cursed them in Albanian. Then, stretching herself up as tall as she could, she walked in through our front door as though nothing had happened.

I ran into our kitchen to tell my father. "Papa, the Serbs have taken the store. They're going to move in there."

My father got up and went to the little Primus stove where he heated his bitter coffee on the countertop. Carefully he poured the thick, hot liquid into a cup and added sugar with a tiny spoon. Then he sat at the table. The whole time, my mother and I were watching him.

Finally he said to us, "Well? Stop your staring. What do you expect me to do?"

Afraid of an argument, my mother filled a bucket with water and began to clean the tile floors in the kitchen with an old pair of pants she used as a mop.

"Mama," I said to her, "they're moving into our house. Can't you at least talk to them?"

"Move," she said. She was on her hands and knees, scrubbing the floor. I noticed how red and chapped her hands were from being so often in water. Her fingernails were short and broken. "Move," she said again.

I stepped to one side. She wiped the spot where I had been standing. Pranvera ran into the kitchen and stood huddled next to me.

"Did you hear me?" I said.

My father sat perfectly still. Since his decision was silence, my mother would go along with it.

She looked up at last. "I will do what I have to do. I have to clean so we can live here."

My grandmother came in then. "Grandma, tell them about the soldiers."

"No. What is there to tell? They are dirty, unwashed pigs. Forget about them and go on with your life," she said. "We'll sell bread from the kitchen instead."

I felt as if I were in a bad dream that was terribly real, in which I was the only one who knew that something dreadful was going to happen. This occurred a lot in the horror movies I watched. One person tried to warn the others, but no one would listen.

I went outside and watched the soldiers move their things in from a blue camouflaged truck parked in front. They didn't have much—just a couple of duffel bags, three cots, and several cartons of food and pots and pans that looked as though they had been stolen from other people's houses. I took a good look at them. One of the soldiers was very young, about the same age as Besim.

"We forgot an electric heater," the tall one said to me. "Go get us yours. I'm not freezing out here in this hellhole. Hurry!"

I went and got the heater, but I didn't hurry. It was our only source of heat besides the small woodstove that heated the kitchen. Doing without it would be one more hardship. I put it down in the doorway to the shop, watching them set up the beds, and then I went out back to the cow shed. Besim was sitting in the corner in the straw.

"What are you doing?" I asked. That was my corner, but I didn't want him to know.

"In a few months, I'll turn eighteen," he said. "Eigh-

teen years old, with three Serbs in the house. My cousin
dead. My uncle beaten."

Thoughtfully he broke a piece of straw in two.

"My father's going to do nothing," I said bitterly.

"Don't speak badly of your father. What can he do
against the Serb army? He is one person. A farmer. And
you act as though he has to be a great warrior. Then,
when he isn't, you treat him with scorn. Everyone can
see how you feel about him, Adem. He's only trying to
stay calm to help you, to keep you alive. Can't you figure
that out?"

He tossed the bit of straw at me. I was stung by his
words and hardly felt the straw hit my cheek.

"I have to do something," I said fiercely. "I have to
change our lives."

He gave a short laugh and looked down, shaking his
head. "Yeah?" he said. "How? How are you going to do
that?"

"Fatmira—" I began.

"Fatmira what? She got herself killed, that's what.
That's what happens if you try to be brave. You get shot,
and everyone else ends up worse than before." Besim
leaned his head back against the cement-block wall,
smiling with bitterness and frustration. "It's hopeless,
Adem. I swear to God, it's hopeless."

Suddenly I whirled around. "Come on," I said. "I want
to see something."

I wanted to see if our house and the village looked the
same now that every breath I took in my house was
changed. I ran out of the shed, then turned left through

the apple trees. Besim ran after me. "Where are you going?" he asked.

Anywhere. I didn't care. "Up the hill." I was out of breath already, scrambling up the sliding pebbles and loose dirt. What little winter snow we'd had was melted except for a dusty white coat on the highest peaks.

We weren't allowed to climb the hills anymore. The border with Albania was only a few miles west. And the nearby border mountains were a no-man's-land, full of lawless smugglers, soldiers, deserters, and thieves, armed men reckless enough to kill anyone who crossed their path. I didn't care. It felt good to be running, climbing. I was so sick of taking naps all the time, of hoping the days and years would go by without my noticing.

"Over here," said Besim. He was following a faint path over the rocks and small patches of grass. "It's easier."

"Is that a fox trail?" I asked.

"Maybe. Maybe deer or goats."

We stopped, panting, at a large, overhanging rock, and by climbing on the boulders at its base, we scaled the side of it until we stood on top looking down at our village. I wanted it to look different, I wanted it to look devastated, but it looked exactly the same even though the Serbs lived in our house with us now. I was scared.

"Besim," I said, "do you think they will shoot us in our beds while we sleep?"

"No. Shut up, Adem. Don't think like that."

"Why not? It's possible."

"Yes, but it was possible before, too. Anyway, this has never happened. Don't even think about it."

"It might have," I said.

"Well, it hasn't."

"How do you know it hasn't?"

Besim looked at me in disgust, then threw a rock over the cliff edge and watched it fall.

"The kids at school say that Prizren will be another Sarajevo. The Serbs have tanks positioned in all the hills surrounding the city," I said, watching Besim's face.

What was I trying to do to him? Make him so angry that he would run down the hill and drive the soldiers out of my house?

Yes. Yes! I wanted him to do that. I wanted someone to do that. Instead my father sat at the kitchen table, and my grandfather whispered curses at the sky above the cornfield so that no one could hear.

"There are no tanks up here," he said.

"How do you know?"

"The hills are too steep even for tanks."

"Okay, not tanks," I said, narrowing my eyes. "Guns and mortars, then. They're going to pick us off one at a time when we go for water, and the whole world can watch us being killed on TV. One at a time."

"Shut up!" he cried. "You're sick. As long as we don't fight back and we keep our solidarity, we're safe. We have to be patient."

"How patient?" I asked, sitting down on the rock and lying my back. "The Turks occupied Kosovo for five hundred years. Is that patient enough, Besim? What good is freedom when you're five hundred seventeen years old?"

He kicked my leg. "I'm leaving."

Up the hill, I heard a cascade of tumbling rocks. Someone was coming. We looked at each other in terror. If it was a soldier, he could find any excuse to shoot us up here. Even if he was a gasoline smuggler, he might shoot us. Frantically, we started to scramble off the big rock.

"Don't worry, don't worry," a man's voice called out in Albanian.

I looked up. One of us? No, a Gypsy. Two Gypsies. I knew one of them—Fikel. He had a string of martens tied to his belt. Gypsies spoke Serbian, Albanian, and Romany, and who knows what else. At least, Fikel did.

"Hey!" I called out and waved.

"It's you," Fikel said, holding up the dead martens by way of greeting.

"This is not a good place to be," the other man said. "What are you doing up here?"

"Then what are *you* doing here?" I answered back.

Fikel burst out laughing. "He's got you there. Are you going to tell him?" he asked his friend.

"The days have eyes, the nights have ears," the other Gypsy replied. He pointed down the steep hill to the village.

This was an old Albanian proverb. It meant that people always knew what you were up to, even in the dark. It was true; we could be seen from a great distance up on the mountain. I hadn't thought of that. I'd only thought of how far I could see.

"Come on."

They waited for us to climb down off the rock, then

led the way down the narrow goat path. A reddish-brown hawk sailed out on the currents of afternoon air. Below, the village looked empty and peaceful. I stared at my house. It looked just the same, but now it was filled with fear and hatred and violence. I started to cry and sat down. The Gypsies didn't wait.

Besim turned around. "Won't you come on? Stop crying," he hissed at me.

"Go ahead. It's not far. Anyway, I want to be alone." I dreaded going back to the house.

"You always want to be alone," he answered, then set off, leaping down the hillside to catch up with the two men.

NINE

At night, I lay in bed, on my sofa in the front room, and I could hear the soldiers on the other side of the wall, talking and laughing. Only the width of one block of cement separated us. They were so bored, they said. Stuck off in some old village filled with cows, goats, and dirty Muslims. They sang songs about killing us and drank a lot of beer to pass the time. They were as bored as I was, but in the opposite way. We were like mirrors through the wall, the reverse of each other.

I tried to keep my eyes open for hours, while Besim lay on his back with his mouth open, asleep. How many times during the endless nights did I long to punch him? How could he sleep so soundly? Then I felt ashamed that I hated my own cousin so much, when it was really the soldiers I hated. That meant they had won. They had turned me against myself. Once I had let hatred into my heart, it seemed to spill over everywhere like a little poisoned stream seeking cracks in the rocks. I didn't know how to stop it.

But what were Besim's feelings? How could he stand sleeping near them? Why didn't everyone feel the way I did?

Often the soldiers got out their guns. Then they went outside and shot them into the air for hours to wake up the whole village. On and on. Bursts of automatic rifle fire. Ten seconds. Fifteen seconds. Then silence. Nothing at all. Meanwhile, my father would come downstairs to watch and wait. Eventually they would stop. Sometimes they shot in people's windows. We all kept away from our windows, but, even so, it was a miracle that no one got hurt.

Other times, they didn't even bother to go out. They shot the guns from inside. How could they stand the noise the guns made? Besim slept through that, too.

During those long nights, I suddenly developed my worst fear, a fear so terrible that I spent hours during the day afraid of the coming night. It came on without warning, without premonition, and it followed me everywhere. I feared that one night, while they were out shooting, they would go to my sister's grave. They would dig her up and then mock her and dishonor her. I was so sure they would do this that I would get up and sneak to the window on my hands and knees to see where they were. It was my fault that Fatmira was left alone, unprotected, not just for now, but for years to

77

come. I laid my head on the windowsill. My body ached with grief.

I lay awake night after night, week after week, all spring into early summer, listening. I wanted them to leave. I wanted us to leave. My eyes had big dark rings around them. I grew even thinner. I hardly noticed when school ended for the year.

"Please, Papa," I begged one morning. "Why can't we move?"

He tilted his head and looked at me. Finally he said, "Where do you think we should go?"

"Albania? Macedonia?"

He snorted. "The border with Albania is closed. You know that. Albania doesn't want us. Why should it? The poorest country in Europe. It has no jobs, no food. And Macedonia? The same thing. Already three hundred thousand people have gone there from Kosovo. The Macedonians want to send them back. And the Greek tanks are lined up, ready to fire at Macedonia if its economy collapses. So what do you suggest? The people who are wealthy manage to escape safely. The rest of us have to take our chances."

Then, before I could answer, he downed his bitter black coffee and went out into the field to work on an irrigation ditch.

"Be patient," my mother said. "That's all we can do. Sooner or later, people will come to help us. We've survived occupations before. We can do it again."

She gave me a chunk of bread and scrambled eggs for breakfast, then went off to try to rouse Besim. I ate slowly because I knew I'd be out in the field most of the morning, helping with the digging. After cleaning the floors in the house, Pranvera would clean the cow shed for me.

I still lived to play soccer. Even though school was out, we played in the school yard with a rock balled up in old socks. One afternoon the soldiers strolled over to the low brick wall around the dirt school yard while we were playing. They leaned their guns against the wall and lit cigarettes. We didn't want to stop playing instantly and show them they had that power over us, but it was hard to play with them watching us. Some Serb boys from the village wandered over and smoked cigarettes with them, commenting on our athletic abilities. It would have been shameful to stop. Instead, I played harder.

Finally the Serbs lost interest and wandered off, all except for the younger soldier, who continued to watch. "So," he said in Serbian, "you are an Olympic hopeful?"

"World Cup '98," I said, diving headfirst for a high shot in the right corner. I landed in the dirt, both knees bleeding, but jumped up and tossed the rock out into the playing area. I wished I were wearing long pants instead of shorts, but it was a hot June afternoon.

The other kids took the opportunity to go home. It wasn't good for us to stay in an organized group for long. Besides, by speaking nicely to me, it could be that the young soldier was drawing me into a trap. Reluctantly I walked over to him. It wouldn't be good for me to be impolite, either. I kept my eyes fixed at his waist level, my face expressionless. We all did that. It was automatic, to keep from getting noticed.

"How old is your brother?" he asked.

"Besim? He's not my brother. He's my cousin. But he lives with us."

"So how old is he?"

I knew he was thinking about the draft.

"How old are you?" I asked.

"Eighteen. I'll be nineteen next month. And?"

"He's still seventeen," I said, not daring to lie. He probably already knew our ages.

We stood quietly together, thinking this over. "What's your name?" I asked.

"It's Gregor."

"I'm Adem." We shook hands like adults.

"What's he going to do when the letter comes?" Gregor asked.

"The draft letter? I—I don't know."

I leaned against the wall. The summer sun had warmed the bricks.

"He'd better have a plan," Gregor said.

"Would he have to go to fight in Bosnia?" I asked. "I heard that's where they send the Albanian soldiers."

"It's possible." He stubbed out his cigarette on the wall. "Cigarettes. What a joke. I didn't smoke until I joined the army. Now I do it to pass the time."

"What did you do when the letter came?"

The question came to me from out of nowhere. Until that moment I had never thought that the Serb soldiers were real people, kids with parents and girlfriends and jobs they no longer went to. The heavy lump of anger I carried inside me released its hold, and I felt suddenly calm.

"I hid at my grandfather's apartment in Belgrade. But it was a stupid place to hide. Someone told on me, of course. Belgrade is a city full of betrayals. The military police came to get me. They took me to the station, and they began to beat me almost at once . . . I chose to be sent to Kosovo, actually. They told us it wasn't so bad here. And now here I am." He cleared his throat. His hands were shaking.

"Why do you shoot your guns at night?" I asked.

He swatted my shoulder. "No more questions. You'll get us both in trouble. Go home, all right? And listen, one day soon, this will all be over. Okay?"

I walked in a daze up the dirt lane, deserted at this hour in the afternoon. Gregor hadn't wanted to come to Kosovo. But still he had done it. And soon they would come for Besim. Was my family so numb and dulled that no one had even thought of this—what to do when Besim's draft notice arrived?

I had read Fatmira's poem so often that the paper was getting soft and worn thin along the fold lines. One afternoon, I sat outside under the apple trees and copied it onto a new piece of paper in my neatest handwriting. Then I took a small piece of dark blue velvet cloth my mother had once used to make a skirt, and sewed a small drawstring bag for it. I wore it on a leather thong around my neck under my shirt, where no one would see it.

I kept it entirely to myself. How could I show something like this to my father or grandfather? And Pranvera was too young. When I thought of showing the poem to my mother, I knew that at the same time I would have to tell her my secret. And I was still afraid to. What if she never forgave me? I couldn't bear the thought of it. I had lost so much already; I couldn't stand to lose her love, too.

One night on television, after the usual propaganda about the new unity between Russia, Greece, and Serbia, there was a short special on "The Ice Man." A hiker had found a frozen body in the Italian Alps. The man had been mummified by the ice for five thousand years.

I crept up close to the TV to look at him. His skin was like leather. It fit tightly to his skull and cheekbones. Next to him were small weapons, tools, and leather clothing that he had been wearing when he died, perhaps trapped by an ice storm. He was grinning in death the way Fatmira had.

Suddenly I was interested in mummification. But there were no books I could look at, no grownups I could ask. The Ice Man had lain in the Alps for five thousand years until that one part of the glacier melted. Scientists could even find food in his stomach to see what he ate. Now bacteria had begun to destroy him. He was decaying, just as Fatmira would. This, too, became an obsession, one more thing I kept to myself.

I was growing afraid of my thoughts—my fear about Fatmira's body being defiled, my obsession with mummies, my fierce anger, my curiosity about Gregor. I borrowed Besim's rock and heavy metal tapes to play all the time. I studied the lyrics, gleeful descriptions of a dark world.

Then one morning in July, I woke up to find that Besim had disappeared overnight. The other sofa was empty—no cover, no pillow. Besim was gone. So were his Walkman and headphones.

I went into the kitchen and stood by the window at breakfast, chewing on a big slab of bread. My parents pretended it was a normal day. Next to me, my father ate yogurt and bread and drank tea, staring idly at the wall. My mother bustled around as usual, even shaking out the carpets, although it was only seven o'clock in the morning and there was no way we could have gotten dirt on them yet. The three soldiers stood outside in the road in their undershirts, smoking and barely awake, scratching themselves under their arms and on their chests.

Out back, our rooster crowed continuously. One of the soldiers pretended to take aim and shoot him. The others laughed.

"Come away from the window. Sit down, sit down," my mother said. "Here. Put on a sweater this morning. You'll freeze."

Freeze in July? I wasn't cold at all. Still I stuck out my arms like a big baby and let her slide the sweater onto me. Then she zipped it up the front while I did nothing. Pranvera washed the dishes. No one said anything about Besim, but I knew they had arranged for his leaving by the way my mother fussed over me.

"Here," she said, spreading chocolate on a second

piece of bread and pouring me a glass of boiled milk from the cows. She had given Pranvera the coating skimmed from the top. She gave me a quick hug and ruffled my hair. I ducked my head away even though I liked the attention. I had my pride to think of.

"He must have gone to Croatia," I said.

No one answered. My mother glanced at my father, but he didn't respond.

"It's two thousand German marks to go to Croatia over the mountains, right?" I asked. "Where did we get so much money? Did we sell something?"

Silence.

I heard my father set his teacup on the table. He wiped his lips extra carefully with the folded cloth napkin my mother handed him. Finally he said, "It's better for you not to know."

His words stung. They didn't trust me. Now I knew for sure that my father liked Besim more than me.

"The fewer people who know about this, the better. It's safer for you that way," he added.

Then he went out to work with the neighbors on the irrigation ditch that would drain into our cornfield. They used shovels the whole time. Later I helped. It seemed as if we had been digging for months, trying to get what little water there was to come down off the mountain and into our corn. It was an endless task. No one knew if we'd ever succeed, but we had to try.

TEN

The soldiers left town one day. No one seemed to know where they had gone or why, although of course we kids all begged Avni to tell us what he knew, until he ran home with his hands over his ears to get away from us.

At first I was very excited. But when I peeked in the filthy window of my grandmother's shop—I saw the room through a film of cigarette smoke, squashed flies, and dried droplets of beer—and realized that their things were still there, I nearly cried with disappointment.

That night, I lay in bed and tried to celebrate by falling asleep quickly. They were gone. I could sleep again without listening to gunfire. Hurray!

In the middle of the night, I woke up anyway. I jerked awake and found myself half sitting and sweaty, as though I'd been awakened by loud gunfire. But I heard nothing. The village lay silent. I wasn't used to it, and I realized it was possible that the soldiers had gone off to prepare a worse future for us.

Don't think that way. You should be happy, I told myself. They're gone, at least for now. Sleep well.

And by the end of the first week, I was sleeping better. When I went outside, I felt full of energy. I wanted to run and play. I begged the kids to get up a real soccer game with a ball and teams like the ones we had in the old days. But no one would.

During the second week, as I lay in bed getting ready to sleep, I began to wonder: Were they really different from us, as everybody said? How could they be? Gregor didn't seem different. He seemed afraid. After all, the military police in Belgrade beat him. He had no choice but to come here.

But how could the other two, especially the tall one who was their leader, do this to us?

One night, I waited until my parents were asleep upstairs. Then I crept out of my sofa bed on the ground floor and into the hall. Moonlight made rectangles on the tiles. Cautiously I opened the front door. I had to see what made the Serb soldiers the way they were. Perhaps there was some clue in their belongings that would explain why they enjoyed humiliating us, torturing us, killing us, year after year.

No one was out in the street at that time of night, but even so, I stayed close to the wall. The door wasn't locked. None of our houses had locks. I opened the door and went inside. A clock sat ticking on the counter where my grandmother used to put the bread. It was two-thirty. One of the cots was behind the counter, the other two in front. There was a beat-up table by the wall, and everywhere there were beer bottles. Mountains of them. The room smelled of rotting beer. I looked under one of the cots, where someone had kicked their dirty clothes. There was a candle on the table for the nights when we had no electricity. There was a battered deck of cards held together by a rubber band. A pack of matches. Crumpled cigarette boxes. But that was nearly all.

I wanted to find a diary, something where they recorded what they'd done each day. I lifted the pillows and looked under the three thin mattresses. What would the diary entries say? Today we beat an old man? Today we beat a schoolteacher? We shot a young girl? There was nothing.

This could have been the room of anyone, or of no one. The soldiers had made nothing of it. There were no photographs of their families—not even of naked girls. It was still my grandmother's bread shop with three beat-up cots in it, and a dirty pack of playing cards. I sat on one of the beds, thinking. So that was how they did it—by not remembering, not thinking about having families just like the ones they were destroying. They did it by drinking beer and waiting for it all to end. They were waiting for American tanks to come, too, just as we were. Then maybe they'd be able to go home.

I heard a car door slam, and a second later a shadow crossed the doorway. I gasped and looked up. They were back.

"Hey! What are you doing? Get out of here!" the tall soldier shouted, enraged. He grabbed my arm and pulled me to my feet and shook me.

"Who is it?" the other one asked.

"The kid next door. Listen, I want you out!"

For a moment I lost my vision, but I managed to have the sense to stumble to the door and hurry back to my side of the house, where I lay awake in fear for the rest of the night. At any moment, I expected them to break down the door and come get me. Perhaps I would be shot on the spot.

I wanted to run upstairs to my parents' room, but I didn't dare tell them what I'd done. I was sure they'd never forgive me for bringing even more trouble into the house. So I decided I would have to do what I dreaded most: leave my family. With wide-open eyes staring into darkness, I decided to run away, and the sooner the better. I knew the soldiers would not forget what I'd done. If I was gone, then maybe they'd leave my family alone.

Now, finally, I had to tell my mother about Fatmira.

I threw back the covers and got out of bed, hurrying across the smooth marble tiles in the hall and up the stairs. My father lay on his back, sleeping soundly. I tiptoed to my mother's side of the bed. She was awake instantly, almost as if she knew I was coming. I knelt down next to her.

"Adem, what is it?" she whispered.

"Oh, Mama," I said, "I knew . . . I knew that Fatmira planned to stand on the bridge and read the poem. She asked me not to tell Besim, so I didn't. But I could have stopped her."

Tears trickled down my face.

"Ssh," said my mother, stroking my hair. "Let's go downstairs."

She followed me back to my bed and covered me with the blanket. Then she sat on the edge of the sofa and continued to stroke my hair.

"It was my fault," I said. "I let her get killed."

"How can you think such a thing? Think of this, Adem. I was the one who encouraged her to write. I was so proud of her. Then why didn't I send her away to study in safety? Why didn't I try harder to protect my own daughter? None of us can foresee the future here. We don't know what will happen to us from one hour to the next."

She sighed and put her face in her hands. We heard a muffled thud as one of the soldiers shoved a cot or table against the wall. She looked up, tense and alert.

"They're back," I whispered. Then I added, "Mama?"

"What?"

I didn't go on. Having the soldiers back was hard enough. In a day or two, I would tell her about my plans to leave, that I would find my cousins in Elbasan and go to high school there.

"Can you sleep now?" she asked.

"Yes," I said. She gave me a quick kiss and was gone.

In the morning, when I got up, I felt tired and edgy. The rims of my eyes were scratchy and sore, and my muscles ached. In a way, though, I felt better than I had in a long time. I went into the kitchen, where my mother was preparing breakfast for my father.

"When's the last time you cleaned out that cow shed properly?" my father asked irritably.

"Yesterday," I mumbled. I should have said that I would do better today.

"Well, do it again, and when you get done with that," he said, "come down to the ditch and help us dig."

I glanced outside. Already, early as it was, the August sun lay hot and flat across the fields, a white glare of light, making the dirt in the fields look pale, useless, and chalky. I made a face. "They're back," I said. "The soldiers."

My mother threw me a warning glance, but it was too late.

"I don't want to hear about it!" my father shouted.

He got up from the table, abruptly knocking over his chair. It fell to the floor with a crash. Pranvera started to cry, I think because she was afraid of the soldiers.

"You didn't think they were gone forever, did you?" my grandfather said. "You should have asked me. I could have told you differently."

"Oh?" shouted my father. "You could have told us differently? I don't want to hear any stories about the war, about the Nazis. There were no Nazis in your house. No Nazis shot your daughter."

Stiff with indignation, my grandfather got up and left the house. He would go to the center of the village to smoke and drink coffee with one of his friends and not come home until dinnertime in a silent feud with my father.

He had had a hard life. Most old people in Kosovo had.

My grandfather had been driven from the republic of Serbia to Macedonia, then from Macedonia to here, near Prizren. He'd been a Partisan in World War II. He had fought against the Nazis with the Serbs—on the very same side! It was the Croats who had sided with Hitler, not us.

My father went out back and got his shovel. He would resume his search for water.

After breakfast, I cleaned the cow shed. Then, instead of going out to help my father, I turned and began to walk the other way, toward Prizren and the Gypsies. The sooner I planned my escape, the better.

It was a long hot walk to the Gypsy camp. Finally I reached it, on the flat stretch of gravel. The trash fire was smoldering. Even on a hot summer's day, Gypsies liked to have a fire going. There was a small truck parked nearby. The back doors were open, so I peered inside. My friend Fikel was there, working on stretching an animal fur.

It was reddish-brown. He held it up.

"You again?" he said. "This is bearskin. There are Russians who still like this. It's beautiful, isn't it?"

"Have you been to Russia?" I asked.

"Sure. Many times. Well, not Russia. Ukraine."

Maybe I could go to Russia, too. "When are you going again?" I asked.

He didn't answer at first. He put down the bearskin and jumped out of the back of the truck, dusting off his hands on his pants.

"Thinking of running away?" he asked.

I stared at him. Was this where Besim had come? I nodded.

"How much money do you have?" he asked.

I shrugged. I didn't know what to say. "How much money would I need?"

"Listen, think about it until, let's say, the end of this month. If you still want to go, then come find me."

He clapped a hand on my shoulder and escorted me to the road.

"Sorry, but letting Albanians hang around my fire is bad news, even for me. Someone might see you here."

When I left his camp, I headed back up the long hill toward my village. As I came around a bend in the road, there, to my dismay, were the three soldiers, standing in the road with their guns.

ELEVEN

We were never supposed to go anywhere alone, but always to stay with someone. I had broken that rule today. Now I was alone, with no witnesses, and from the casual way the soldiers were standing in the road, I knew my moment had come.

Still, I kept walking toward them, my face lowered, my eyes fixed somewhere about three feet off the ground. My face was expressionless, although my heart was pounding and my knees were shaking. Just keep walking, I told myself. Act as if nothing's wrong. Stay calm. Don't let them sense your fear.

That was what the grownups had told us. Stay calm. Cooperate. Don't argue.

"Hey, kid! Hold it," one of them said.

I stopped. They began to walk toward me. Would Gregor dare to help me? I glanced up at his face, but he wasn't looking at me. His face, too, was a complete blank. The other two were laughing.

"Well, if it isn't the little soccer champ!"

I blushed and looked down.

"Since when has Yugoslavia let Albanians onto the World Cup team?" They all laughed at their cleverness, even Gregor. "Hey! I asked you a question. When?" the tall one said.

"Never," I said in a low voice.

"So, champ, where's your brother?" the taller one asked.

My brother? I was confused for a moment.

"You heard me. Where is he?" The soldier gave me a hard shove. I staggered backward.

"Besim is my cousin," I said, "not my brother."

"I don't give a damn who he is. I want to know where he is."

He poked the rifle under my chin and lifted my head up so that I had to look at him. To my shame, I had begun to cry out of fear, but at least I managed to cry silently. I glanced again at Gregor.

"Don't look at him, idiot. He's not your buddy anymore. We're going to straighten that out. Where is he?"

"I don't know!" I cried.

"Of course you know. We need soldiers to keep Yugoslavia together for the Serbs. We can punish anyone who disrupts the unity of Greater Serbia."

He jabbed the barrel of the rifle into the soft place below my Adam's apple, and I fell down. Then he stepped on the fingers of my right hand with his army boot. I could feel the crunching of my bones. "I don't know! I don't!" I cried.

"What's this?" he asked.

When I fell, the leather thong and velvet pouch had slipped up over the neckline of my T-shirt. The soldier reached down and pulled it off me. He tore open the little bag.

"A love poem. Isn't that sweet?" He crumpled it up and threw it on the ground. I was glad he couldn't read Albanian.

"Whether or not you know where your brother is, we've decided you're a troublemaker. So we're going to teach you a lesson for coming into our room. You're a spy for the Alliance, no doubt. Clever of them to use a kid."

"No!" I screamed. "I'm not!"

This is it, I thought. They're going to shoot me. I am going to die here in the middle of the road, the way Fatmira did. They will carry my body home, and my parents will go crazy with grief.

The other one took out his pocket knife, opened it, and slit my T-shirt from top to bottom. Gregor turned away so he wouldn't have to watch. They joked about castrating me. Suddenly Gregor whirled around. "Shut up, you pigs!" he yelled.

In that moment, I jumped up and started to run away, but the tall one tackled me by the legs and threw me to the ground. I was sobbing and thrashing now, out of control. They stood on my arms. "Do you know what a Serb cross is?" they asked. The shorter one bent down and began to carve my chest. One large Orthodox cross with the Cyrillic "S" in each corner for the saying, "Only unity saves the Serbs."

I felt the slow, hot sting of the knife as the blade drew its thin red line across my chest. It took forever to carve the four "S's." They talked about cutting off my nipples because they ruined the design. In the end, they drew smaller crosses above each one. They stood back, laughing and surveying their handiwork while I lay in the road, their boots still pinning my arms.

"Now you will carry our cross for us." They laughed. "You're an Orthodox icon."

They let me go. Shaking uncontrollably, I scrambled to my feet, left my T-shirt and Fatmira's poem lying in the dirt, and stumbled down the road, then crossed a ditch and ran into a field. I threw myself on the ground, crying. I should have run farther, I thought. Perhaps they would come into the field and kill me. At that point, though, I didn't care. All I felt was shame and a sense of my body having been violated. I wondered for a moment if that was how girls felt after they had been raped. I had been marked for life.

I sat up and glanced down at my chest. It was streaked with pale mud and with blood. I couldn't tell how deep the cuts were, but the bleeding seemed to have stopped.

I had forgotten for a moment about my hand, but now I remembered. My middle three fingers, which the soldier had crushed with his heavy boot, were throbbing with pain. Any slight movement, and the pain shot through my hand, up into my arm. I began to cry again. I was sure my fingers were broken.

I rubbed at my cuts with my left fist, stupidly thinking I could wipe off the cross. I wanted to find some way to get rid of the marks before I went home. I pulled some leaves off the cornstalks and spat on them, trying to clean my chest, but I only smeared the blood further. Finally I gave up and lay on my back, staring up at the harsh blue sky.

I wanted my father to get a gun and kill them. All of them, even Gregor, whom I'd thought was my friend. Maybe in a way he was. But, like my father, he was helpless. I knew that now. Speaking out had brought Fatmira her death. And in trying to make sense of everything, I had been attacked. I had no doubt in my mind that next time the soldiers would kill me. My father was right not to confront them. The odds against us were way too high. We were completely trapped.

The politicians told us the world was listening, but how did we know for sure? What if it wasn't? The world hadn't listened to Bosnia, we all knew that. The world had betrayed Bosnia most of all. It had watched thousands of Muslims get killed. So why would it listen to us? We weren't even dead yet.

I rolled onto my side and drew up my knees, still crying. How could I face my family like this? I could imagine their horror and grief when they saw me. I knew they would rush to clean my wounds and put a shirt on me to cover them. Then, worst of all, we would go on as we had before, day after day, year after year. My family would be in danger every one of those days because of me, because of the cross.

I lay in the dirt, waiting for evening.

I wouldn't live my life like this, I swore to myself. My parents had to stay behind to help Halil, Pranvera, my grandparents. But I could help my family best by leaving. Only then might the soldiers leave my family alone.

The sun went down behind the mountains, and cool, purple shadows spread across the field. Swallows darted and swooped for insects. Two white goats grazed unattended in the ditch. A car went by, then a truck, raising a cloud of dust. I heard the steady clop-clopping of a farm cart heading for town. The soldiers had disappeared.

Just over the Sar Mountains, in the direction of Macedonia, a bright star appeared. I was shivering miserably with cold and loneliness. Remembering Fatmira, I began to feel some of her strength, her bravery. I could hear her laughter, and I saw her hopeful, excited eyes. I wanted to pull her spirit into mine so that I could be stronger, so that one day I could start to be the "many voices" from the poem.

I stopped crying and watched the star gleam more and more brightly as the sky darkened from a deep turquoise to inky black.

I was afraid to go home, afraid to cause my parents more grief. I knew they would be horrified. I worried most of all about my father. I couldn't go home. But, after a while, I did.

TWELVE

I stood in the back doorway of the kitchen while they were clearing away supper.

"Where were you?" my father roared, and raised his hand to smack me before he'd even noticed.

Pranvera ran in front of him and threw her arms around me. My mother saw the blood and moved Pranvera aside. I stood like a doll, my limbs as stiff as plastic. My mother crouched before me, looking at the cross, her hands to her face. Then she whirled away to the sink and brought a wet cloth. "What happened, Adem? What happened to you? Who did this? Was it the soldiers?"

I nodded. She started to clean off the dirt. The water was cold, and I flinched.

"Don't," I said. "I'm hungry."

"Make some tea, Pranvera," my mother said. My

father was swearing and pacing back and forth. He glanced again at my chest and hurried out of the room. I saw that he was crying.

My mother sat me in a chair with a blanket wrapped around my shoulders and gave me hot, strong tea with mounds of sugar in it and a thick piece of bread.

In no more than ten minutes, my father came back with two older men, Halil Raziri and Beqe Shukriu, who had been the elected officials of our village before the mass firings. They pushed back the blanket and examined me, while I stared at them over the rim of my teacup, trying not to shiver.

"We must get him to Prizren as soon as possible," Raziri said. "We can arrange for a car."

"No! He shouldn't go anywhere right now," my mother said. "Look at him, how cold and tired he is. He needs to rest."

I didn't care what they did to me. I felt as if I were in my own dream and couldn't wake up.

A car came a few minutes later. My father told the Democratic Alliance men to wait outside. He took me by the shoulders and wrapped the blanket tightly around me, his eyes full of tears. I wanted to say something to comfort him, and I could see that he wanted to do the same for me. Instead he pulled me to him and gave me a tight hug. Then my mother and I were bundled into the backseat of the car under the watchful gaze of our three soldiers. I tried to catch Gregor's eye, but he kept his face turned away so I couldn't.

"Ask your Albanian doctor if he knows what that

cross means," the tall one called out as we climbed in. "And tell him every boy in the village will be wearing one soon."

"Take care, now," the other said, slamming the car door for us. "Bon voyage. Say hello to the Western journalists!"

Our driver swore to himself and drove off hurriedly. Soft music was playing on the car stereo, not the usual Albanian nationalist folksongs but a gentle-sounding jazz. If only I lived in that place, I thought, the place where that soothing music was made. I could live there and be content.

As we passed the Gypsy campsite, I peered out the window. A large bonfire of burning trash sent orange sparks drifting up into the black sky. It hardly seemed possible that I had been there earlier that same afternoon, that it was the same day. I didn't see Fikel.

We drove down the long hill toward the sparkling lights of Prizren in the narrow valley. At the bottom was the usual roadblock. The police were stopping cars. I shuddered when I saw the police and drew in my breath. My mother gave me a hug, but they waved us through without stopping us. We were a little bit lucky for once.

Our car twisted and turned through narrow little streets, hundreds of years old and crowded with pedestrians. Finally we stopped, and our driver jumped out and banged on a large oak door set in a cement wall. The door opened a crack, and I saw him explain that we needed to come in.

The driver helped my mother and me out. We were whisked inside by the guard, then led across a cobble-stoned courtyard and down a passageway. We went through another door and up a flight of stairs, into a room lined with sofas and low tables. A group of five tired-looking men in suits were seated around one of the tables.

"Come over here," the man at the head of the table said. "How are you tonight?"

It was Dr. Dedusha. He took me by the shoulders and pushed the blanket back. He looked carefully at the cross.

"I am Dr. Dedusha. Do you remember me from the time I visited your home when your father was in jail?"

I didn't answer, but my mother nodded. "Yes," she said.

"And he is the brother of Fatmira?"

"Yes."

Dr. Dedusha stood aside then so that the other men could see me. I stood there, half-naked, tears swelling in my throat, my face scorching hot, my hands icy cold.

"This happened this afternoon?" he asked. "At what time?"

One of the other men slammed his hand down on the table and jumped up. "Never mind that. This is too much. We can't stand for this. Are we going to sit back and take every single ounce of abuse they dish out?"

I was shivering and wanted to put the blanket back on, but Dr. Dedusha held my shoulders. With my hands hanging down like that, my right hand throbbed terribly.

"We have to stay calm. There is no other choice!" Dedusha said.

"There is a choice, by God. The choice is action. For over five years we've let them shoot us, torture us, starve us. Now they can carve up our children with knives, and still we say nothing? We do nothing?"

"We will do something, Mustafa. They are bringing a camera right now. This boy's photograph will go out over the news wires. It will be in the Western papers. The diplomats will read of this. I assure you, we are doing something. We are," Dedusha said.

The other man, Isuf Mustafa, snorted with derision and lit a cigarette. His hands trembled.

"Please," said my mother, "don't argue now. Not in front of my son."

The two men ignored what my mother said. "Listen," Mustafa said in a quieter voice. "The people who do these things are not calm. They are not normal. If you want to put it that way, fine. They do not think with reason. They recognize only violence. We've tried diplomacy and resistance for years. It was important to try. But now they are grinding our faces in the dirt. It is past time to react, Dedusha."

Now it was Dr. Dedusha's turn to slam down his hand. The loud noise scared me. "No! In open warfare, we would be destroyed. We would be forced to fight our Serb neighbors. Besides, the military has moved in with us. We would be massacred just like the Bosnians, only worse, because we have more children and no weapons.

In resistance, we can keep our dignity and we can survive."

"I don't agree!"

Just then the door opened. We all turned to stare at it. It was the guard from the main entrance. He had brought a camera. He glanced at Dr. Dedusha for permission to take my picture.

"Yes, yes, go ahead," Dr. Dedusha muttered.

They turned me to face the camera. I felt the dream feeling in my head again, but stronger than before. Behind me the voices of the men buzzed angrily as they argued. My eyelids felt heavy. The light flashed in front of my face, and I fainted.

Later, I dreamed that the camera was a gun.

I remember waking up at some point and seeing my mother. I tried to sit up.

"Ssh," she said gently. "Just rest for now. You were exhausted." I lay back and someone gave me an injection in my upper arm and everything went hazy. I could hear people's voices, but their words made no sense. Then I slept again.

I must have slept right through the whole next day. When I woke up, it was night again. I glanced down at my hand. A splint on my fingers helped to immobilize them. They didn't feel nearly as painful.

I lay still for a few minutes, thinking back to the argument between the two men the night before. Dr. Dedusha had often come to our school, urging us to stay calm, to stay quiet in the face of abuse. But maybe Mustafa was also right. Maybe there was a time to fight back.

I heard a knock at the door.

"Come in," I mumbled.

The door opened. A different guard opened the door and ushered in two foreigners, one with a camera and bag. Journalists.

"Hello, lad," said the one without the camera, stepping forward with his hand outstretched to shake hands. British.

"We heard about your situation and we're very sorry. We wondered if we might have a word."

I looked at his hand for a moment, mystified. At first I thought he wanted me to give him money. Then I realized he was being polite. I didn't like British accents. In school, we all tried to speak in the American way we heard on the videos.

I got out of bed and stood up. My stomach rumbled and I felt dizzy, maybe from the injection that had made me sleep. Why had the Democratic Alliance put me to sleep? Where was my mother? What if Dr. Dedusha was really a Serb spy? I had heard people say that before, but I'd never paid any attention. Now it seemed possible. Anything seemed possible.

The photographer fiddled with his camera. The other one got out a little notebook and sat on the edge of the bed. "Is this all right?" he asked.

Why did he keep asking me things? I had no idea of the answers. When I didn't answer, the photographer gave him a warning glance as if to say, "Maybe this one's not too smart."

"Can you tell us what happened yesterday?"

Still I didn't answer. If I told him, worse things might happen to my family. Surely the Serbs would be furious if I actually spoke to Western journalists. I was afraid now in a way I never had been before. I didn't trust these two men. Why should I? I thought it entirely possible that now the Serbs would try to find an opportunity, an excuse to kill me. That was what I was thinking about, not what British journalists wanted.

"They said he speaks English very well," the photographer said. "Listen, let's just take his photo. We can interview someone at the Alliance later on."

"Right. Hey, do you mind if we take your photo? It's all right if you don't want to talk about it. We can ask someone else. Could you just lift up your shirt a bit?"

I didn't move. All I could think of was my family. No matter what I did now, in this room, I would betray my family and cause them harm. If I spoke to the reporters, the Serbs would be furious. They might come back to our house and perhaps kill my father. Yet if I didn't speak to the reporters, the world would never know what had happened to us here in Kosovo. I would be betraying the resistance. But I couldn't risk the safety of my family on the slim chance that I would be helping the Alliance.

"Listen," said the photographer, "we're here, so lift up his shirt. I'll take one quick shot and we'll be out."

"Right."

Very gently, the British journalist lifted the front of my shirt. It was a man's shirt, large, white, with buttons down the front and the sleeves rolled up. Perhaps it had belonged to Dr. Dedusha.

"Jesus," the photographer said. "Poor kid."

I peered down at myself. The cuts were an angry red now, swelling on either side of the hard, brown, scabbed lines. Someone had cleaned off the mud. The flash went off, and I blinked and sat down on the bed.

The reporter bent over me and put his hand on my shoulder. "I'm sorry, lad, I really am. We'll do what we can to help."

But I wasn't listening to him. Outside, I heard a car drive up, then another. Several doors slammed. I glanced nervously toward the window. The photographer quickly shoved his camera into his bag. "Let's go," he said. "Come on."

That was the first time I realized that they'd put themselves in danger to help me. I heard shouting outside and went to peer out the window. Two military jeeps were parked on the narrow street that was more like an alley. The jeeps entirely blocked the street. The journalists had come with a car and driver. A group of special police were pushing and shoving the driver and asking him who was inside.

Fear rushed through me. I looked at the two British journalists, who still didn't realize the full significance of what was going to happen. But I knew. I knew and I wasn't waiting around. Besides Fatmira, eleven other children had been shot in Prizren.

I wasn't going to become the next.

THIRTEEN

I opened the bedroom door, ran along a short hall, down the back stairs, and out into an inner courtyard, separated from the street by a high cement wall. I climbed onto the roof of a tool shed and scaled a second wall, then jumped to the ground. I was now in a courtyard that opened onto a different side street from the one where the jeeps were parked.

I stood in the shadow of the wall and tried to think what to do next. If I went home, I was sure I would cause more trouble for my family. If I didn't go home, there was the possibility that this would all settle down and eventually they would be in less danger. I couldn't go home, I'd already decided that anyway. Now it was simply more urgent. I had to leave right away.

I made a quick decision. I would go to Fikel and hope for the best. I knew that the Gypsies owed allegiance to no one, neither Serbs nor Albanians, and that they might inform on me as well. But maybe because I had already talked to Fikel, he would help me. Maybe. Then I would try to reach my cousins in Elbasan.

It would be dangerous getting to the Gypsy campsite because of the police roadblocks. I would have to go through the vineyards.

I lay down on the ground to rest until I was sure that the jeeps and reporters had gone. Then I climbed the wall and began to thread my way through the crowded back alleys of nighttime Prizren.

I passed two roadblocks right away. The police were out in force tonight, stopping and checking many cars, but they didn't notice me as I walked quietly past them on the dirt edge of the narrow street up against the courtyard walls. Even so, my heart was pounding, and in my head I prayed to God, Muslim, Catholic, and Orthodox —all three, just in case—to spare me and keep me safe.

Finally I reached the outskirts of town, where the vineyards began. I stepped through a hole in a wire fence and, keeping low, started to climb the hill, staying parallel to the road. I was worried about the visibility of my white shirt, but I knew I would need whatever clothing I could find to protect myself against exposure if I made it into the mountains, so I didn't dare get rid of it.

I was high enough on the hillside now so that Prizren looked like a narrow carpet of lights. Above me the stars hung low, with ice-blue light. I thought of how ancient they were, but constant, seen by me now as shepherds through the centuries, standing on these hills, had seen them. The rays of thin blue light seemed to reach across time and pierce my body, connecting me to the earth. I loved Kosovo.

Maybe that was the only thing my father wanted—a very simple thing—to be able to stand in his field and look at the stars at night and think about the centuries rolling past. I hadn't understood. I'd criticized my father too much because he wanted to stay in Kosovo.

Ahead of me, a fox barked once and scampered off to his den. The foxes loved to eat ripe grapes fresh from the vine. It had been nearly two days since I'd eaten a regular meal. I stopped to try some of the grapes, but they were hard and very sour. They'd ripen in September.

It took me about thirty more minutes to reach the campsite. Although it must have been well after midnight, the campfire was still hot. I could see the orange glow of embers through black ashes. A dog barked. He'd been sleeping by the fire, but now he came forward, slinking low to the ground and growling. I held out my hand and talked to him softly. I was afraid he might bite me.

"Go lie down!" a man's voice shouted.

Fikel had climbed out of the back of his truck, rubbing his face sleepily. "You again," he said. "In the middle of the night, this time."

I nodded, unable to speak. I didn't know how to begin to tell him what had happened to me in the short time since I'd last seen him. But I knew Fikel was patient.

Two women, one old, one young, appeared.

"What's going on?" the old one demanded. "Who is this boy?"

"Never mind," Fikel said. "I'll handle it."

The older woman smacked the dog on his nose, and he lay down again near the fire. I would rather have been that dog, even when he was hit, than myself at that moment. After they left, I stepped closer to the fire so Fikel could see and pulled up my shirt.

When Fikel saw the Serb cross, his head jerked back just a little and he pressed his lips tightly together. But he said nothing. No one in the former Yugoslavia ever gave an opinion if he didn't have to. It wasn't safe. We were all used to dictators and informers.

"I have to run away," I said. "Not in September. Now."

"Did you bring money?" he asked.

I shook my head. "No."

"Can you get some?"

"No."

I felt dizzy with fatigue and nervousness. I just wanted to lie down. "If you can't take me, then let me rest," I said.

"Come on," he said, and helped me into the back of the truck. I climbed inside and lay down on a pile of animal skins. Fikel sat in the opening. I could see the dark rise of the hill and mountains beyond, then the stars above his head. He lit a cigarette and leaned against the side of the truck. I went to sleep.

Judging by the glare of the sun and by the heat, I woke up late the next morning. The first thing I felt was fear: not nervousness but blind confusion. I jumped up and went to the truck's open doors. I couldn't believe that I would be able to escape the Serbs by walking away, yet, at the same time, it seemed completely possible. I just wished it were over, that I'd already done it. I didn't know if I had the strength to really go through with it. I was so close to home that I longed to see my family one more time, but I didn't dare.

The campfire was burning high, and the air smelled strongly of rotting garbage. I didn't see Fikel anywhere, but I saw the old woman sitting in a plastic lawn chair in the shade of her caravan, sewing. Even in the August heat, she wore a stained pink nylon windbreaker and long pants. The heavy, garbagy smell didn't seem to bother her at all. The dog that had growled at me lay under her chair. I knew I had to find something to eat. Maybe I would feel less confused on a full stomach.

The old woman looked up and saw me and pointed to the fire. There was a kettle sitting on the ground. I jumped out of the truck and walked over to the fire. The kettle was full of rice, bits of meat, and scallions. Half a loaf of bread sat on a cutting board on a second lawn chair. Quickly I tore off a big piece of bread and wolfed it down. Then I helped myself to the rice. The dog got up from underneath the chair and slowly approached me with his head outstretched and back flat. I held out a chunk of bread. He seized it and trotted back to the safety of the lawn chair.

Then I noticed a bear. Chained to the rear axle of Fikel's truck by a ring through his nose was a small brown bear, a yearling cub. He was sitting back on his haunches, testing the pull of the ring through his nose, jerking his head up and back in a careful attempt to get loose. I was surprised at how intelligent he was.

I got up to go pat him. He was round and still cute, about the size of a large sheepdog. But as I got closer, the woman yelled out, "No!"

I glanced at her. She shook her head warningly. The bear had turned toward me and was watching me carefully, swaying lightly on his front feet.

I was angry that Fikel would keep the bear tied up like that. I wanted to free him immediately. Without going any closer, I tried to check the chain to see how it was attached to the truck. It was looped around the axle, then clipped together with a large padlock. I got down on my hands and knees to look under the truck. The chain was heavy enough that there was no way I could force the links apart.

There was nothing else to do but wait for Fikel. I fretted anxiously about what my family must be thinking about me. I wanted to send them a message, but not until I was over the mountains and safe. For now they would know from Dr. Dedusha that I had gotten away.

All morning I waited, but I didn't dare stray far from the truck for fear of being seen. Finally, around midafternoon, I saw Fikel walking slowly up the long hill from town, carrying two plastic shopping bags. As he neared the camp, he gave me a quick smile. He brought the bags over to the truck.

"Hello," he said. "It's hot."

Sweat trickled down his forehead and the back of his

neck. His black hair was damp and curly. He pulled a bandanna out of his pocket and wiped his face.

"Tonight," he said, "we'll go. You and I with the bear cub."

"Is he yours?" I asked.

"For now. I'm taking him over the mountains to my cousin in Albania. There is a much better price for bears in Italy than in Bulgaria, let's say. I was going to keep him around for another month. Then he would be a little bigger, a little fatter. A better price. But, since you are here, we'll go now."

Fikel reached into one of the plastic bags and pulled out a liter of Coke. He lifted the bottle and toasted me in Albanian. *"Gëzuar,"* he said. "Be happy!"

After taking a long drink, he passed me the bottle. *"Gëzuar,"* I replied, my voice catching a little. The toast reminded me of happier times with my family, when we were all together with my cousins and grandparents.

"The problem is," Fikel said, "that bears eat a lot. And there's not much for a hungry bear to eat in the mountains."

Then he turned and looked at me. "The other problem is you—how to get you past the police. You'll have to leave here, anyway, so it might as well be tonight."

He looked at me calmly and took a large drink of soda.

I felt a thrill of fear run through me. Why had I trusted him? He could easily have betrayed me to the Serb authorities in Prizren today. Perhaps they were already coming for me.

"There are a lot of roadblocks up today, so I have made

arrangements for a Serb driver to take you and the bear through your village. Meanwhile you'll be hiding. I think you are thin enough to fit behind the seat or, better yet, in the trunk. I will sit the bear up front. He will provide a very good distraction."

Fikel grinned at me. He had no teeth in the front, and his skin was wrinkled and very dark from a life outdoors. When he smiled, he looked much younger than I had thought him at first. "Ready for an adventure?" he asked.

"Yes."

"Good. Let me see what you have for a knife."

"A knife?"

"You aren't carrying one?" he asked, truly surprised. He looked disgusted and climbed into the truck to search for one.

"I didn't have time to pack," I said.

Fikel hooted with laughter. And for the first time in what felt like years, I laughed, too.

FOURTEEN

After sunset, a small man about thirty years old, in stained jeans and a leather jacket, drove into the campsite in a little Russian car the color of chicken broth. He got out and strode over to the fire as if he thought he was a cowboy.

"*Dobro vece,*" he said. A Serb.

He shook the old woman's hand and then came over to me. I didn't get up to greet him. I was still sitting near the bear cub. At that point, the bear was letting me scratch beneath his ears the way I used to scratch my cow. I remembered my cow for a moment and hoped Pranvera would take good care of her.

"Let me see," the Serb said.

I gave him a sullen look but lifted my shirt. He whistled. "And your fingers, too?" he asked.

I nodded. I couldn't bring myself to talk to him. He crouched down on his heels and placed his hand on my head. "I want to tell you something before you go," he said. "We are not all like this. Remember that. Tonight I will do what I can to help." Then he paused. *"Mirë!"* he said.

It was the first time I'd ever heard a Serb use our language. I was amazed. *"Mirë,"* I said happily. Good. Then in Serbian I said, *"Da."* Yes.

He turned to Fikel. "Let's go," he said.

He unlocked the little trunk of the car and gestured with his head for me to get in. Fikel handed me one of the plastic bags. It was filled with bread, packs of cigarettes, and some chocolate and a bottle of soda. I had a knife that Fikel had given me, a switchblade, in my back pocket.

"You can fit," the Serb said. "You're skinny enough. But I'm warning you, it's going to be a bumpy ride. From the village, we'll be going down a farm road and then along the stream, where I'll let you out."

I waited to see the bear get in the car. Fikel unchained him, but he was unwilling to go. Fikel put a piece of chocolate on the seat to tempt him. Finally I went over to the bear. He was scared, that was all. By scratching him under his ear and talking softly to him, I got him into the car.

"What did you tell him?" asked Fikel.

"Just that I know what it's like to leave home."

I climbed into the trunk. The Serb slammed it closed. Instantly I panicked. What if this were a Serb trick and they never let me out? Or what if they were going to return me to the police for money? What if there was no air in here and I suffocated? I should never have trusted anyone.

The car started to back up. I smelled exhaust leaking in through the lining of the trunk. I tried to control my rising panic by slowing down my breathing. Maybe I would die in here and this trunk would be my coffin. I thought of Fatmira, how I might not be able to visit her grave for years to come. I thought of how one day she would rot and her bones would become soil. And a farm horse, maybe one just like ours—white, with bony hips and a yellowed mane—would someday plow the earth by her grave for planting. It felt wrong to leave her, maybe even more wrong than leaving my parents and Pranvera and Halil. But I no longer worried that the soldiers would hurt her. They had come after me instead.

The exhaust fumes gave me a headache, and the bumping of the car over the rutted roads jarred my teeth, so that I bit my tongue hard. I tasted blood in my mouth.

Now the car was driving more slowly. The bumps were longer and softer. The car rocked from side to side. We had to be crossing the fields on the way to the river. I pressed my face up against the plastic opening where the taillight was. I could feel a small stream of fresh air leaking in around the plastic. But it was pitch-black in the trunk. The Serb driver hadn't turned on his lights.

Finally the car stopped. I heard the front door slam. Keys rattled in the lock to the trunk. The lid lifted, and, overhead, I saw the stars in the cloudless night sky. I felt suddenly hopeful.

"Hello!" I said to the driver in Serbian. "How are you?"

He shook his head as he pulled me up. I climbed out of the trunk and took a few steps to get the kinks out of my legs. The Serb slammed the trunk shut.

"I'm going now," he said. "Good luck to you."

He shook my hand.

I'd trusted him this far. Could I trust him to reach my parents?

"Please," I begged, "can you tell my parents that I went to Elbasan?"

He glanced at Fikel, trying to decide what to do.

"If not my parents, then just tell an Albanian from my village. Please."

He nodded.

"I will see you again," he said to Fikel.

Then he got into the car and drove off, and Fikel, the bear, and I were left standing by the alder bushes that lined the shallow stream skirting the base of the mountain.

"Come on. There's no point in hanging around here."

Fikel and the bear strode off ahead of me, and I hurried after them, carrying my plastic bag in my good hand. There was no moon, and I had trouble seeing in the dark. We had started to climb the mountain on a long diagonal. My right foot kept slipping on small rocks, and twice in a matter of minutes I twisted my ankle.

"I can't see," I complained.

"You'll get used to it," Fikel replied. "But we need to hurry. The nights are short enough."

Tucking the end of the plastic bag under my belt, I

stumbled after him, keeping my left hand low to the ground both for balance and so I could feel the rocks better. We were high enough to see the lights of Prizren and even a few lights in our village. My parents must be worried to death about me, but soon they would know that I was on my way to Albania. Albania, then maybe someday the rest of Europe or even America. That was the first time I'd actually let myself think of where I was going, and that I might really get there.

We'd been climbing for nearly two hours. I was out of breath, exhausted, and my knees ached and trembled with fatigue. I turned and looked back down the valley. My village had disappeared. Prizren was gone. Ahead of us, the dim outline of mountain peaks rose sharply above our heads.

"Can we stop?" I asked.

"No," said Fikel shortly.

But I was in luck. A few minutes later, the bear sat down and refused to budge. With relief, I sat down, too, and patted him. Fikel opened a liter bottle and poured Coke into the bear's mouth. When the bottle was empty, the bear got up and moved about restlessly, looking for more, swinging his head back and forth and sniffing. He poked at my plastic bag with his claws.

"He smells the cigarettes," Fikel said.

He let go of the chain and let the bear paw about on the side of the mountain.

"Where did you get him?" I asked.

"I shot the mother. It wasn't far from here. You saw the bearskin in the truck? That was her."

I laid my head on my drawn-up knees.

Fikel sensed my unhappiness. "I have to live," he said. "Life is hard for all of us here."

I nodded.

"Look at the bear snuffling around the rocks. I think he may sense we are near his home," said Fikel.

"Who put the ring in his nose?" I asked.

"I did. It's the easiest way to tame them. Little bears learn quickly to follow you and not argue. Once you reach Elbasan, my cousin will take the bear on to Durrës, where they can cross by boat to Italy. A healthy cub is worth quite a lot of money."

"He's smart," I said.

"Yes," said Fikel, stubbing out his cigarette on a rock. "Bears are very intelligent. They can be taught to ride a bike."

In spite of myself, I had to smile.

"But don't get too fond of him. This cub is our money for the winter."

I felt sad, but I knew what he meant. No one kept pets anymore in Kosovo. How could they when there was so little food? When a stray dog came into the village, most of the kids chased it away, throwing stones and sticks at it.

"Come on, we're trying to reach one of the flint caves by early morning. Have you seen those before?"

I didn't know what he meant. Since I'd been ten, it had been too dangerous for children to explore the mountains. Fikel picked up the bear's chain.

"Flint is the stone that holds fire. People dug into the

cliffs to look for it. We'll hide there by day. Usually I am not nearly so careful, but, for you, anything. Come on."

At our backs, the sky had turned light gray, streaked with pink. It was nearly morning. We slid down a steep escarpment covered with loose stones into a bowl-shaped depression. In the dawn's light, I could see several hollowed-out areas carved into the rock face. Fikel, leading the bear, chose the middle one of the three and ducked inside. I followed.

The floor of the small cave was littered with shattered bits of rock. There was just room enough for us each to lie down and stretch out, as long as the bear didn't get restless. But he plopped down onto his stomach and promptly went to sleep like a young dog. As soon as he was asleep, I helped myself to a chunk of bread and a few swallows of Coke, trying not to think about how hungry I felt. The bear snored louder than a drunk soldier.

"I'm going to sleep, so listen. We are right near the border with Albania," Fikel said. "Border patrols—both Serbs and Albanians—will be looking for trespassers. So don't go wandering off. You'll be very sorry if you do. We are right near the place where the Albanians are selling gasoline to the Serbs. You know how many people have died up here this year? Forty."

Fikel lay down with his head on his jacket. "Hey," he said, "if something happens to me, find my cousin. His name is Teo."

I managed to sleep for several hours. When I woke up, it seemed to be about midday. I pulled up my shirt to look at my scar. The redness around the cuts seemed pinker and less hot. The bandage around my fingers was filthy, but I didn't dare take it off. I traced the Serb cross with the fingertips of my good hand.

What had Fikel meant when he said Albanians were selling gasoline to Serbs? That was impossible. The Albanians felt solidarity with those of us in Yugoslavia. They wouldn't break sanctions like that, selling gasoline that could be used to run Serb tanks and army jeeps. Would they?

At school, everything had been explained to us: who was wrong and who was right. How the Albanians would never betray one another, that one day we would have a united Albania and all the Albanian people could then be together. This was our national dream. Unfortunately, the Serbs had the same idea for Serbia and would do anything to make it happen.

But last night a Serb I didn't even know came to help me escape. And because I had been scarred with the cross, Fikel was helping me, even to the point of risking his life. We were a fragile chain of people who barely knew one another, stretching out our hands, reaching back into darkness and danger to help. None of us needed to ask questions. Everyone understood the dangers. Forty people dead. Shot. Some trying to escape, some trying to make money. I wondered if I would ever make it to Elbasan.

Fear made me dizzy. I closed my eyes.

Oddly enough, the bear seemed to adjust his habits to ours quite easily. He still slept soundly after our night of walking. It would be hard to let him go with Teo to Durrës and let him be sold to a circus or roadside zoo. I had seen bears in captivity before. Their faces were dulled and sad, their fur dirty and matted. People hit them and laughed at them. But I understood that Fikel wanted to help his cousin.

The afternoon wore slowly on. It grew very hot in the flint cave. The sun's glare on the rocks out front was bone-white. The shadows on the dark sides of the rocks looked black and indistinct. I sat in the cave opening and memorized every boulder—its contours, shadows, and shapes.

Suddenly the sky seemed to roar, a roar so loud that it sounded as if the world had been ripped in half. I looked up and saw the flash of a Serb MiG-29 clear the top of the mountain by only a hundred feet. The Serbs were probably strafing Prizren today. They did it sometimes, to scare us.

I crept deeper into the cave and hugged my knees to my chest, praying to all three Gods that I'd make it safely into Albania.

At one point, far off, I heard automatic rifle fire. Twenty seconds. Then again—twenty seconds. We were not alone up here, no matter how deserted the place looked.

FIFTEEN

Finally Fikel woke up. He sat up and tried to stretch his arms in the cramped space.

"So," he said. "Tonight we will meet my cousin. We're near Lake Guri. It's located half in Albania and half in Serbia. It's one of the lakes that the Albanians bring the gasoline to. Then they use boats to bring the gas into Serbia."

I was annoyed that he called this place Serbia, when rightfully it was Kosovo. It was my homeland.

"My cousin will meet us in a small grove of olive trees on the far side of the lake just before morning. The trees each have a small circle of white stones around the base to try to keep the soil from being washed away. You can see the stones in the dark. Pay attention to this because it's possible that we may become separated. If we do, try to find the olive trees."

I frowned. "How do you know your cousin will be there?"

"He's there every night," Fikel said.

"You mean he brings gasoline for the Serbs across the lake?"

"Yes."

"Then he's a traitor!" I shouted angrily. "The world has sanctions against the Serbs."

"Quiet! He's no traitor. What do you expect from him? How is he supposed to survive? You and I are one loaf of bread away from starving. But so is he, and many other people."

"It's wrong to sell them gasoline. It goes to tanks and weapons in Bosnia and Kosovo."

"Gypsies owe allegiance to no one. We're nomads. We own no land. This war, and every other war like it, has been caused by Albanians and Serbs because they want to own each other's land. That is the problem. The problem is created by Albanians, Croats, Serbs. Not Gypsies."

I had to be quiet then because it was true. For centuries, people had been slaughtering one another in the Balkans for land. But no war had been started by the Gypsies.

"It's those who claim to be nationalists who are wrong, who kill all the people," Fikel said. "Not those of us who sell bearskins or small tanks of gasoline and cigarettes so we can eat."

So Fikel thought I was the enemy.

"Then why are you helping me?" I asked finally.

"Because you came to me," he said simply. "You

needed help, and there was no one else you could turn to. Otherwise you would have, before you would have asked a Gypsy."

That was true, too, I was ashamed to acknowledge. We looked down on Gypsies. Everyone did. We called them dirty, backward, and lazy, just what the Serbs said about us.

"I'm sorry, Fikel," I said.

"For what? You're a good boy. You don't know any different. You haven't traveled the way I have. I have more freedom than you in that regard."

"Have you ever been to America?"

"No. But I have been to Italy, Hungary, Slovakia, Ukraine. Once I went to southern France. Also to Turkey and Greece."

"Bulgaria?" I asked.

"Yes. And Transylvania."

I laughed. We had talked about Transylvania before.

"Can you read?" I asked.

He spat. "How many Gypsy children go to your school?"

"None," I admitted.

"Well, there's your answer, then. Besides, what good has reading done you? The Serbs took all your books. What is there to read?"

Fikel handed the bear a dry sausage and poured him a few swallows of Coke. The bottle was almost empty, and I was dying of thirst. I tore off a chunk of bread, but my mouth was so dry that it was very difficult to swallow. I would drink the lake water as soon as I got the chance.

"We'll follow the south shore of the lake," Fikel said. "My cousin checks for me in the olive grove at dawn. He waits about thirty minutes to see if I am coming that day."

We lay on the rocks, listening to rounds of rapid gunfire echo off the mountainsides from someplace that I hoped was far away.

After the sun went down, we still had to wait nearly three hours before Fikel thought it was dark enough to set off. We climbed straight up the mountain above the flint caves, then crossed a narrow, saddlelike ridge to the south.

Now I could see the lake down below. I saw small white lights moving unsteadily along the north shore.

"Serb border patrol," Fikel said.

"There are no lights on the Albanian side."

"They think it wiser not to check the lake too often. Albanians wait until there is plenty of money around for them to get a big, fat bribe. Then they check," he said.

The bear munched on some leaves and twigs from low bushes. There were no trees anywhere. There was one chunk of bread left. I split it with him. He nudged at me with his snout, hoping for more. I showed him my empty hands.

"We'll keep moving along the shore. Let's hope the border guards will be watching for boats and not for us," Fikel said. "Come on. It's nearly three miles."

I groaned. After the long climb last night, my feet were

sore and my ankles ached. I felt dizzy with hunger and had trouble keeping my balance. We stumbled on in the dark for nearly two hours.

We had come down the slope of the ridge and were now much closer to the edge of the shore. From the lake I could hear the whine of boat engines bringing the illegal gasoline across, but they sounded far away. I began to feel confident that my escape was almost over. It could only be another mile, or two at the most.

Suddenly I heard a dog bark a sharp warning. The bear gave a low growl and swung his head from side to side, trying to catch the scent of the dog.

"Get down," whispered Fikel. "Stay very low."

He handed me the bear's chain.

"Can you bribe them?" I asked.

"I have no money. They'd take the bear. But don't worry. We can wait until they go by."

But the dog barked again. Three sharp barks. Then I heard men's voices in Serbian. "Up here, I think. Let me check."

"The dog smells the bear," whispered Fikel. "Okay. I will give myself up and negotiate with them. Keep the bear here. It may be that I know them. Don't move. Don't leave this spot, whatever you do."

"Why don't you just let the bear go?" I didn't want Fikel to leave me hiding in the rocks alone.

"Are you crazy? The bear is worth thousands of German marks. That's a lot of food for my family."

Fikel crawled forward, then, stooping, half ran, half slid down the side of the hill toward the shore. I heard a clatter of stones as he cried out. "Don't shoot!" he called in Serbian. "Don't shoot! I'm not armed!"

I heard the frenzied barking of the dog, then a burst of automatic rifle fire. Loud voices. Then gunfire again for fifteen seconds. It seemed endless.

Crouched low behind a boulder, I moaned and shoved my fist into my mouth to keep from making any noise. I was sure they'd hit Fikel. I was sure he was dead.

I could hear the voices of the two men on patrol. They were arguing about what to do with Fikel now that he'd been shot. No one could survive fifteen seconds of automatic rifle fire, I knew that. I heard them say that he was only a Gypsy, so it didn't matter. The dog barked sharply once or twice.

"Shut that dog up, will you?" one of them said. "We don't need to do anything with the body. Let his relatives find him. Someone's bound to come looking."

They argued a while longer, then moved off northward around the shore of the lake. I waited and waited to be sure they were gone. Then I crept out from behind the boulder and tugged lightly on the bear's chain. He got to his feet and padded after me. I tried to prepare myself for what I was sure I would see.

I found Fikel's body lying on the rocks. His head was twisted sideways, and he was looking up at the night sky. All the bullets had hit him in the upper body. The Serbs had had time to practice their marksmanship. Beside me, the bear whimpered, then lay down.

Tears spilled from my eyes. I sat next to Fikel, filled

with fear and sadness. It seemed to me that the bravest people suffered the most. They put themselves in danger to help others, never thinking about what might happen to them along the way. My sister had died for a river. Fikel had died for me.

Now I didn't know what to do. Apparently, I still hadn't reached the Albanian border. But it had to be very close, which was probably why they'd shot Fikel. I couldn't stay where I was. Much as I hated to, I would have to leave Fikel lying here until I could get a message to his cousin.

Still I didn't move. The whine of the boats crossing the lake had finally stopped. I watched the stars slowly crawl across the sky until a cloud bank began to obscure them, snuffing out the stars one at a time. It must be nearly morning, I thought.

I felt a few drops of rain on my face, and I could see the raindrops leaving pockmarks on the surface of the water.

I took off my white shirt and laid it over Fikel's up-turned face. Then I anchored it with a circle of stones. I turned to the bear, who was resting next to me, and tried to rouse him. "Wake up," I said, shaking him. He curled himself tighter and kept on dozing. "Come on. We have to go."

I got to my feet and tugged the bear down to the lake's edge and let go of his chain. I stared quietly into the clear lake water. In that one moment, looking through the water, I felt my body shift and relax. For the first time since Fatmira had died, I saw that one true moment when the bullet hit her back. I saw the rabbitlike twitch of her body just before she fell. Instead of frantic anguish, I felt a soft and gentle sorrow. And the pain of leaving behind her grave and the soil that held her bones loosened its hold on me.

I scooped up handfuls of cold water and splashed my face. Then I sat back on my heels.

I carried Fatmira's poem inside me now, and it helped me to go on. It was wonderful that she had tried to speak out. I still felt lonely, leaving Fatmira and now Fikel, but it was a soft, knowing loneliness I could wear like a coat. Now when I remembered them, I could feel warmth that was like the warmth of home.

I waited patiently for the bear to drink the cold water from the rocky edge of the lake. Because of Fatmira's bravery and Fikel's generosity, I knew that I would make it to Elbasan. Then, someday, I would return to Kosovo and read my sister's poem aloud.

"Come on," I urged the bear. I grabbed his chain and gave it a shake.

In the faint light of early dawn, he scampered beside me, his fur rippling and rolling with his stride, as we turned and headed south along the shore toward the grove of olive trees.